THE SHAPE
I GAVE YOU

THE SHAPE
I GAVE YOU

MARTHA BAILLIE

ALFRED A. KNOPF CANADA

PUBLISHED BY ALFRED A. KNOPF CANADA

Copyright © 2006 Martha Baillie

Knopf Canada and colophon are trademarks.

www.randomhouse.ca

LIBRARY AND ARCHIVES CANADA CATALOGUING IN PUBLICATION

Baillie, Martha, 1960–
The shape I gave you / Martha Baillie.

ISBN-13:978-0-676-97748-6
ISBN-10: 0-676-97748-0

I. Title.

PS8553.A3658S5 2006   C813'.54   C2005-905405-0

First eight lines of "At a Certain Age," used as epigraph to Part One, from
New And Collected Poems: 1931–2001 by Czeslaw Milosz. Copyright © 1988, 1991,
1995, 2001 by Czeslaw Milosz Royalties, Inc. Reprinted by permission of
HarperCollins Publishers. Ecco Press. The epigraph to Part Two comes from
"String Practice," from *Robinson's Crossing* by Jan Zwicky, Brick Books, 2004.

Text design: Leah Springate

First Edition

Printed and bound in the United States of America

2 4 6 8 9 7 5 3 1

For Mary Jane Holmes Baillie, my mother.

THE SHAPE
I GAVE YOU

PART ONE

We wanted to confess our sins but there were no
  takers.
White clouds refused to accept them, and the wind
Was too busy visiting sea after sea.
We did not succeed in interesting the animals.
Dogs, disappointed, expected an order,
A cat, as always immoral, was falling asleep.
A person seemingly very close
Did not care to hear of things long past.

CZESLAW MILOSZ, "At a Certain Age"

Standing at the corner of Leopoldstrasse and Theodor-strasse, waiting for the traffic lights to change, Ulrike curled her toes to warm them inside her boots. She turned her head to the left and looked in through the window of the Kosmopolit Beauty Salon, where a middle-aged woman sat in a white chair, holding out her hands. The beautician was saying something and smiling as she examined her client's cuticles.

A girl, no older than five, installed in the chair nearest the window, was occupying herself by drawing a picture on a large pad of paper. The child was going at her work with utmost concentration, eyebrows scrunched together, pencil gripped between her small fingers. Ulrike took a step closer and, with her forehead nearly touching the glass, looked straight down at the girl's drawing. It was of a boy with large ears and dark, serious eyes, a thin boy holding what was either a shovel or a butterfly net in his hand. Ulrike looked up. Both the beautician and her client were staring coldly at her. She stepped quickly away from the window.

The light changed and she hurried across Leopoldstrasse, the child's portrait of a young boy and the disapproving faces of the two women trading places, back and forth, in her mind. She arrived at the streetcar stop. By now it felt to her as if all the cold in the city were gathered in the skin of her left cheek, in a spot the size of a pfennig. She rubbed at this spot with her mittened hand. The brilliant, freezing air gave even the ugliest buildings, the concrete monstrosities from the 1960s, those that used to so offend her father, a newness, a sharp eagerness. The streetcar was scheduled to arrive in ten minutes.

To escape the increasingly loud, embittered exclamations of a man standing at the streetcar stop, clutching his cellphone to his ear, Ulrike opened the door of the nearest café and was about to go in but thought better of it. Unless she succeeded in positioning herself in the window, she might just miss the streetcar. She stepped back outside, fished in her pocket for a tissue and blew her nose. The man at the streetcar stop put his cellphone away and started to cry. When, Ulrike wondered, was the last time she'd seen a man weep?

In the window of the café, perched on a bar stool, elbows propped on the high narrow counter, a slender blond girl, seventeen or eighteen years old, with thoughtful eyes and a ring in her nose, was reading a book. Though the book's spine faced the window, when Ulrike tried to read the title she found she couldn't. It was in Greek. A young man came and stood beside the girl, who set her book down and kissed him on the mouth.

For an instant, Ulrike was opening the heavy wooden door of the shop where, at seventeen, she had bought her sheet music. She was leaning over the counter and, in full view of any customer who chose to notice, planting a kiss on the skinny neck of the boy behind the till.

The streetcar arrived and Ulrike climbed on. Perhaps the man had not been weeping, his small blue eyes merely watering profusely because of the cold. He now sat opposite her, reading the newspaper, sturdy, with a cleft in his chin and a grey moustache that seemed out of place, it had been trimmed so small. As the streetcar glided forward, Ulrike decided which book to take with her on the train to Düsseldorf the following morning. In Düsseldorf she would give a recital, a balance of Bach and Schubert, and teach a master class. She felt well prepared, comfortable with the Bach. Her final, critical hours of practice in the morning had quieted her nerves. She'd set this afternoon aside to relax and make any small but necessary last-minute arrangements. Her errands done, she was now free to go home. On the train tomorrow morning she would read Ian Rankin's *Mortal Causes* to keep up her English.

She glanced at the man seated opposite her. His eyes were dry. But his earlier sorrow had been real. She must call her agent straight away, she told herself, and agree to play, despite her dislike of politics, at the Green Party benefit in Frankfurt at the end of April. She must also phone two of her students to reschedule their lessons. Packing her clothes for Düsseldorf should be quick. She'd reward herself with a hot bath. More snow was expected for tomorrow. Tonight she'd dream.

Whenever she left Berlin to play in another city, her sleep swelled during the night preceding her departure. It released dreams, surprising as flying fish. A month ago she'd set out to

7

give a concert in Rome, followed by a second in Florence. The night before her departure, she'd found herself riding in a train headed for Geneva. Just as the truth dawned on her, that she was being rushed through the wrong countryside, the train came to a sudden stop in a field planted with sugar beets. She stepped down from the train. She walked between the rows of leafy plants, across the field, toward a burning house of a suitable size for a doll. When she reached the house, she went in. Nothing was charred or smelled of smoke, the white walls looked clean and women with soft, heavy thighs and breasts, who might have escaped from a painting by Rubens, danced from room to room, waving diaphanous scarves about. In the yard behind the house a wooden crate stood on the ground. She knew what was expected of her. She knelt beside the crate. She waited. Soon the gladiator would come and cut off her head. He arrived, but equipped with only a twisted, rusty scrap of metal, a tool clearly inadequate.

Whatever she dreamed tonight would be less disturbing. Approaching concerts in foreign cities of importance might bring on a burning house, buried sweetness under a leafy field, nudity and the threat of losing her head, but Düsseldorf was not a demanding engagement. One recital, a class to teach, then home again. The hall where she'd be playing was modest in size, with good acoustics, and the piano was one she liked.

She stepped from the streetcar into an assault of cold air. It was a short walk to her building, through the incoherent mumblings of the city, through the precise chop-chopping of a man clearing ice from the sidewalk in front of his shop. She pressed in the numbers of the code. As the buzzer went off, she pushed the door quickly open. She took out a small key and opened her mailbox. Into its narrow interior a bulky padded envelope had been stuffed. She yanked the envelope out. She turned it over. It was plastered with Canadian stamps. But I don't know anyone in Canada, she thought; and then the mockingly familiar handwriting corrected her.

Beatrice Mann
139 Clinton Street
Toronto, Ontario
M6G 2Y4 Canada

Ulrike Huguenot
Chodowiecki Strasse 42
Berlin 10405
Germany

January 15, 2003

Dear Ulrike Huguenot,

I am writing to you because my daughter has died. But this explains nothing. You must be wondering why I'm addressing myself to you. My name is Beatrice Mann. What does my name mean to you? What do you know of my connection with your father? Your name, Ulrike Huguenot, means a great deal to me.

It is not my daughter's death I'm going to tell you about, but something else, a series of events that concern you more directly. I want you to judge the evidence, to decide what connections exist.

Ulrike, I'm going to use your first name because "Ms. Huguenot" would sound ridiculous, though it would be a relief to place some distance between us. Between me and what I did, for years, with a willingness to harm you.

I wonder how old you are now? That depends, I suppose, on when you receive this letter. It will take time to complete. Perhaps I am writing in order to begin.

I may lock this letter in a drawer and not send it. In which case, it isn't you I'm speaking to but myself. I expect, however, that once this letter fully exists I'll not be able to resist mailing it to you. I hope my German isn't too awkward and that you'll grasp what it is I'm attempting to say.

You are twenty-eight today, if my calculations are correct. When you receive these scribblings, it will be up to you to choose what to ignore or to disbelieve.

You and I first met in your parents' living room on Nürnberger Strasse in Berlin. Do you remember? You were fourteen and rolled on the floor with your younger sister, Ingrid, wrestling. Was Ingrid twelve? The blinds were closed and the room felt small, though the walls were painted a light, agreeable colour. The piano consumed most of the room. A painting by a Polish artist hung on the wall—a frame within a frame and nothing in the centre but a copper smudge. The frames were made of paint and text, most of the overlapping words illegible, thank God. If a painting must include text, the presence of the words should constitute their principal meaning.

I'm thanking God, without knowing if he exists. My daughter is dead.

You must know the painting? That one by the Polish artist, in your parents' living room. What do you think of it?

We were waiting for your father, Gustave, to arrive. I was a bit surprised but pleased that your mother didn't ask you or Ingrid to get up from the floor. Your wildness relieved us. There we sat, your mother, Isaac and I, she and I especially anxious, waiting for your father. It was as if our nervousness had spilled over onto the floor, and you rolled in it, pulling and laughing. My husband, Isaac, was the most relaxed of us all.

Isaac and I had come to Berlin with our daughter, Ines, who was only four at the time. We'd come because Isaac's photographs of the sites of postwar camps for displaced persons in Augsburg, Bad Worishofen and München were included in a show at the Werkstatt für Fotografie in Kreuzberg.

The opening of his exhibit had proved far more successful than he'd dared to hope, and now we were free to enjoy Berlin for a few days, pleasantly buoyed by the very real prospect that Isaac might at last receive some recognition when he got home. "It's always the way for Canadians," he was explaining to your mother. "Once your work attracts attention in some other country, then the galleries at home wake up."

It was Ines, our daughter, who said at last, "I can't concentrate with all this rolling around." She was seated at a small table, drawing. She voiced her one complaint, then concentrated on her work. You and Ingrid stopped wrestling, sat up and looked at her. "What did she say?" you asked in German. She'd spoken in English. She was small for her age, articulate and determined, an only child. Visibly, you were both intrigued by her, you more than Ingrid.

I was grateful to your mother for having found and brought in the little table and chair, perfect for a child of four. There was a hope the evening would go well. Isaac seemed contented, and Ines was happily engrossed in her work. Isaac and I would be free to talk, to listen.

Your mother was dressed entirely in white, her shirt made of silk, her pants perfectly pressed. Her hair resembled your father's, dark, wiry and abundant. Her eyes were the scene of a bright, contained struggle. I don't think I'm inventing this. I remember her eyes—their lively intelligence, their intriguing shape—and the struggle. Between vulnerability and pragmatism? Between rebellion and acceptance? Had she guessed that I was in love with your father? Had she decided to accept me all the same?

—

Your mother was waiting for him, as usual. She glanced at her watch and said, apologetically, "Gustave should be here soon. He said eight, and it's half past." She offered Isaac another vermouth and told him she'd found the glass filing cabinet in the centre of his installation quite fascinating.

"Private and public memory—you've taken on a lot, the immense displacement of people at the end of the war. Your doorways and empty courtyards seem, to me, a bit chilly. They're exquisite, of course, but rather cold. Not that I don't like the subject you've chosen. I do, and you're right about memory. It's slippery, elusive. It's all very rich." Evidently, she added, she was not the only one to think so. It had been a wonderful turnout.

I agreed with her. Except that I didn't believe Isaac had chosen his subject. It had chosen him.

I looked up at the ceiling and saw how high it was, then felt, again, the smallness of the room. I hoped, Ulrike, that your father would arrive soon and take charge, give us all a reason for finding ourselves together in a small room.

"And your work?" your mother asked me. "What is it like? Can you describe it?"

I hesitated.

"Forgive me," she added. "I'm asking you a difficult question. How can a sculpture be put into words?"

Your mother's mixture of graciousness and honesty filled me with admiration. I thought again how kind she was to have dug amongst your old things, yours and Ingrid's, to find the little table and chair she'd brought in for Ines. I tried to answer her by describing clumsily the sculptures I'd been sanding and painting until the day before we left Toronto for Berlin. The challenge of explaining my work distracted me from thoughts of your father.

Your mother stood up because the tip of her cigarette was turning to ash, and she found a little metal ashtray on a side table, then balanced herself on the arm of her chair, both restless and tired but eager to listen, and knocked the ash from the end of her cigarette silently into the vessel cupped in her hand.

"About a year ago," I explained, "I drove into northern Ontario and found six large, abandoned stumps of freshly felled trees, which I brought back south with me. The largest stump measured six feet in circumference. I believe most trees are merely cut down, but some are murdered. It's a question of intention."

"Intention." Your mother turned the word over in her mind, considering my claim. "Yes, intention plays a part. And the result? If I kill someone by accident or on purpose, is that someone differently dead? Yes, I think the result as well as the action differs. Not all deaths are the same."

I explained that I'd hollowed out the stumps and then gouged deeply into the exterior of the remaining ring of wood, trying to recreate the tread of a tractor's tire, that I'd sanded, then painted my fake "tires" black.

"I want people to believe," I said, "that they're looking

at discarded rubber, the remains of a machine, until they touch one of the rings and their hand tells them, 'Wood! These were once alive.' For those who don't touch, I'll provide an explanatory sign, hung discreetly on the wall. I want people to experience the shock of realizing they've been fooled and, while thrown off balance, to start thinking about industrial production. What is the lifespan of rubber? Of wood? I want each tire to be beautiful. Into some I've carved deep treads; others I've smoothed, as if the tread were worn away or the rubber had melted. They're simple. As simple as the ring of bone that's left when you've eaten a pork chop, only very much larger, large enough an adult could slip through one. I hope they echo the eternity of bones. I intend to place them on their sides, set well apart, so that people can look or crawl through them. They could be giant wedding rings."

"They must be very powerful, these huge, hollowed-out tree stumps, disguised as rubber tires, as beautiful rings. You haven't any photos?" your mother asked.

"Not with me."

"What a shame. Perhaps one day your sculptures, like Isaac's work, will be shown in Berlin and I will be able to walk between them and look through them?"

"Perhaps."

I hadn't seen your father in fifteen years, Ulrike. However, much more recently, barely a year before our trip to Berlin, I'd got up my courage and sent him an invitation to an exhibit of my work being held in a small

Toronto gallery. I knew he would not attend. For him to have come from so far would have been absurd. It was an excuse to send him something, to remind him of my existence in the form of a dozen sculpted heads stuck on wire stems, photographed and made into an invitation. I waited for his response to my odd bouquet and received none. Then, at the opening, the owner of the gallery handed me a slender cream-coloured envelope. "This arrived for you yesterday." I tore the envelope open. Gustave's praise raced across the page. His voice was in my ear. My work pleased him. It delighted him. I folded the fine sheet of paper quickly, stealthily as a child catching a cricket, slipped my prize into the pocket of my skirt. We never believe we'll receive what we want the most. I wiped a sudden sweat from my palms onto my skirt, reached for a glass of wine and turned to speak with an acquaintance who'd come to see my show.

And now, here I was, seated in your parents' apartment on Nürnberger Strasse. Every piece of furniture in the room felt acutely present, the black piano, the small brown velvet sofa where I sat beside Isaac and waited for your father to arrive, the gold and green chair occupied by your mother, the empty blue chair waiting for your father, the leather stool you got up from to disappear into who knows what other room, closing the door behind you, leaving your sister sprawled on the carpet at our feet—and against the wall, your father's desk.

When I'd walked in, I'd glanced down and seen his name on an envelope. This is the desk where he sits and writes, where his thoughts take shape. If I touch his desk, I'd wondered, will I ever be able to pull my hand away? It was untouchable.

I started writing this letter to you a few hours ago, Ulrike. I came upstairs and opened my studio door. I call this room my studio, though I have a larger space I rent in what was once a warehouse downtown.

Isaac is in his study across the hall. As his door is closed, I can only guess at what he's doing. Sorting negatives or drafting a letter to the director of a museum or checking his e-mail. Perhaps he's staring at the wall, as I was doing, downstairs, until the necessity of this letter grew in me. Maybe, as I was doing, he's picking mindlessly at the dead skin on his lip to see if it will bleed. Or else he's set everything aside and is reading a book on theories of beauty and the role of photography in the postmodern era. I hope that he's succeeding in concentrating on something other than Ines; I hope he can think of no one but her.

When I came upstairs, I was carrying the start of this letter inside my head, determined to speak to you. There is a detail concerning Ines' death that I cannot bring myself to reveal to Isaac.

Isaac has just brought me a cup of tea. "I'm going to cook some dinner," he told me, as he set the cup down. "I'll call you when it's ready." He is being kind, but I am not hungry. I have no desire to leave this room.

I don't expect that you remember Isaac very well, from that one evening in your parents' apartment.

I have made a mistake, Ulrike. Nürnberger Strasse was not the first place you and I met.

Once, when you were only six, I stood with you in the hallway of your grandmother's house above the village of Rolle. I was staying with your grandmother on my way through Switzerland to Italy. You, your parents and your sister, Ingrid, were living in Geneva that year. You shook my hand. Your hair was the colour of hay, not dark like your parents'. It was neatly combed and shone.

I went to my room, fetched a bag of pink candy-coated almonds and handed them to you, explaining, "These are for you and your sister." Your father reached out and took the package. "I'll do the dividing," he said with a wry smile. I felt suddenly ashamed. The bag looked so small. The dividing done, you and Ingrid would end up with a paltry six nuts each—six nuts covered in hard pink sugar. I had not thought. Neither of you were real. You were children. I had none of my own and no intention of producing any.

I'm mentioning this incident because I want to set everything in order, to leave nothing out, and because I still feel quite badly about not having offered you a more generous gift.

Chronologies, Ulrike. Do you enjoy order? I find it a relief. At first, I find it a relief. Events precede each other. Precision is possible.

Not fifteen years since I'd last seen Gustave but eight. You and I meeting for the first time in Switzerland, not Berlin, and your father snatching up the bag of pink candied almonds to distribute them fairly. Order is a bare hill with a view. The valley opens below.

But whenever my life has become too orderly, I've reached for chaos. As if the strongest truths must be extracted from some chemistry of confusion.

What events pointed my daughter in the direction of death? Decades of them, or none?

Ines got on her bicycle and rode down l'avenue du Parc in Montreal. She'd lived for eighteen years. A passing car knocked her over.

I first met your father when I was seventeen, one year younger than my daughter was on the day she died. Your father, how shall I refer to him in this letter? Can I say to you, simply, "Gustave"? He was not yet your father when I first met him.

I was spending the month of August on an island with my parents. The island belonged to our family. An ancient, worn, shattered rock rising out of Lake Huron. White pines grew from its wide pockets of soil. Not the twisted specimens of the outer islands that I considered beautiful and my father scoffed at. The pines on our island grew straight and tall as ships' masts, formed a true woods whose dense heart was shunned by the sun. This woods and its rocky clearings stretched between the island's two bald granite tips.

I often complained of the mainland's proximity, of its ugly, oversized houses lining up along the steep shore. On calm days the mainlanders' voices and their insistent music floated over.

My father explained to me that during the war, from the deck of a British destroyer, he'd seen enough open, endless water to last him a lifetime. For this reason he'd chosen a protected island, one near a mainland that had not yet been developed, not back then, when he bought the island.

Our cottage was a wooden tent with a glass front. It overlooked the bay, its back to the pines. Our feet on the plywood floor made a hollow sound. Under the floor, open air hung or swam, depending on the weather, and beneath all that—the rock.

We unstrapped our watches, forgot to wind the little clock with the cracked glass face. Wind moved coldly at the top of the pines, while a warm inebriate stillness of dead needles, lichen and moss spread out at our feet. The days lapped at our differences, smoothing, rounding them. In the hottest noons we held ourselves still in order to examine the comforting precision of a pine cone, the fallen piece of sandwich, a snake's fine tail.

Then suddenly I was seventeen and restless. The house having never been completed, our clothes hung from nails. Undressing, at night, observing my long, ungainly, imperfect body, I remembered jumping, when I was small, from the exposed girders, through firelight, onto my bed.

Though seventeen, I'd not yet rebelled—not against my father. My parents were older than those of my friends. My friends were few. On weekends my parents took me away with them to the countryside, and summers we spent on our island. I'd adapted to my rather isolated existence.

When cool, damp weather took us indoors, my father or I made a fire. No doubt my mother constructed and lighted some of those fires. I don't remember.

My father had fought in the war, and I respected him for having suffered and survived.

Whereas my mother, what proof of heroism could she offer me? At some point in my childhood, I don't recall when, I'd decided I did not want to resemble my mother. Her indecisiveness and lack of ambition, a certain wariness or vanity, the emotional equivalent of wearing dark glasses indoors, these traits I held against her. I was being quite unfair.

Ulrike, your father once told me that you were strong in mathematics and that you also possessed an uncanny, intuitive understanding of people. What a rare combination. It was you at sixteen he was describing: "She's of another era. Ulrike knows she is different from her contemporaries and appears to accept the consequences of this."

A year or so later he mentioned in a letter that you'd been admitted to the Universität de Künste Berlin and had chosen the piano as your vocation. "I am proud of her. She has proven she possesses tenacity as well as talent." I wonder how your father would describe you to me today. In a Christmas card your grandmother sent to me several years ago, she said that you were recording a CD. Congratulations. I'd love to hear you play. Please tell me the title of your CD, so that I may look for it.

But this is inappropriate. I apologize. I am writing to you because I want you to judge me. And surely it is not advisable for me to attempt to form a friendship with my judge? You may say that you cannot judge me. But we all do judge each other. We must.

The driver of the car was speeding and came too close. His side mirror knocked Ines. She couldn't have saved herself. Possibly, the gods took my daughter's life to punish me, to punish me for my relationship with your father.

Ulrike stared at the page in her hands. She was standing in her narrow, sunlit kitchen, furious questions igniting inside her. How dare she? Who does this woman think she is? She must be suffering from some sort of psychotic breakdown. Does she truly think I'm interested in her obsession with my father? If her daughter is dead, then I ought to feel sorry for her. What does she want from me? I don't have time for this.

Her outrage growing, Ulrike examined the number penned in the upper right corner of the page she was holding. Page 15. I've read through less than a quarter of it, she thought. She felt tempted to rip the pages into long, jagged strips. But then I'd have to fit the torn bits back together in order to keep reading, she warned herself, and to avoid behaving rashly she set page 15 down. "I haven't time for this," she repeated under her breath. She tried to stuff the bulky letter back into its envelope. Several pages lay askew. She banged the letter, slapped its sides, lined up everything. It slid into place.

She carried the weighty envelope through to her living room and stood, looking for somewhere appropriate to put the thing. No appropriate place existed. She set the document on top of her piano. There it lay in full view while she telephoned her agent. She accepted the invitation to play at the Green Party benefit, though in her present mood she no longer wanted to. She called three of her students and rescheduled their lessons. Her music bag stood propped against the leg of the piano bench. She opened it and looked inside. Everything she'd need in Düsseldorf was waiting, packed and ready. She glanced at the top of her piano. The envelope, far from having disappeared, had grown, if anything, larger and thicker than before. It contained thousands of words, each word as carefully applied as an acupuncture needle. Who does she imagine she's curing? Herself or me?

A sudden squealing of brakes freed Ulrike from her thoughts. Turning her back on the envelope, she looked out the window, down into the street, but nothing in particular was happening outside and she turned again, to be confronted by her sofa and the blanket covering it.

The blanket was a villager's, sent to her from Rajasthan the year before by her ex-lover Thomas, who'd rushed off to India in search of spiritual purity and in order, Ulrike believed, to escape from her, from her refusal to produce a child with him. The blanket was woven of a rough wool that repeated washings had failed to soften. The previous summer, she'd folded it away because it scratched at her bare legs, and at the skin of her friends' legs. But by mid-October, her legs no longer bare, she'd brought it out again. The blanket said a lot about Thomas, and it was hers, and it belonged on the sofa.

She sat down, and straight away her cat, lean and grey,

drifted into the room. He leapt onto her lap and settled, surprisingly warm and solid, tucking his front paws neatly under his chest. His name was Darjeeling. She stroked the fur between his ears until a voluptuous rumbling climbed from deep in his throat. "Mutti will come once a day to feed you while I'm away," she told him. She shut her eyes and concentrated on the opening aria of Bach's *Goldberg Variations*. She could hear exactly how she'd play it tomorrow, in Düsseldorf. But suddenly her playing was interrupted by the appearance, in her mind's eye, of her mother's face hovering in profile, above a large fern. Her mother set aside her watering pitcher and glanced down through her living-room windows into Nürnberger Strasse. "This street, at least, is still recognizable," she said, pulling a pack of cigarettes from the pocket of her cardigan.

Ulrike had stopped by Gerda's earlier in the week. She'd scrutinized her mother for signs of loneliness. But Gerda did not appear to be lonely. She published articles, taught several courses, navigated departmental politics, went regularly to the theatre with friends, travelled and attended concerts and parties. She led a life far busier, less solitary, than that of many women half her age.

"What will you play?" Gerda had asked.

"Schubert and Bach."

"Which Schubert?"

"The Moment Musical #3."

"Ah, so you're doing mostly Bach, then?"

"*The Goldberg Variations*."

"You've given yourself quite a lot. But you'll carry it off. Where will you be staying?"

"Same hotel as last time. The one with the overactive heating system that makes all the rooms feel tropical. But I'm used to that. In my building they either crank up the heat or turn it off altogether. The hotel serves good breakfasts." Ulrike picked up the bag containing the new boots she'd just bought at Rippen's, in the next street over. "I must get going. You're sure you don't mind looking after Darjeeling?"

"I don't mind."

"Thank you. Thank you, Mutti. Next time I'll try to find someone else."

"Darjeeling and I get along very well together. We, at any rate, are good friends," said Gerda. She walked with Ulrike to the elevator, where they kissed each other goodbye. Ulrike rode down inside the little cage, accompanied by Gerda's seemingly insignificant remarks, *This street, at least, is still recognizable* and *Darjeeling and I, at any rate, are good friends.*

Some people, my sister, Ingrid, for example, thought Ulrike as the elevator arrived at the ground floor, are quite adept at protecting themselves from the emotions of others. I am not.

Ulrike got up from the sofa. This is not how I planned to spend my evening, she told herself. My clothes aren't packed, and I've no idea what I'm going to have for supper. Max said he wouldn't come by, as he has a rehearsal. I want to take a bath, a cool bath. It's far too hot in here.

The obstinate envelope lay on top of her piano. Her mouth felt uncomfortably dry. She walked into the kitchen, into the incongruous, jarring rhythms of an Elvis Presley song.

Her neighbours across the courtyard had their windows thrown open, despite the bitter weather. Their apartment must be as overheated as mine, Ulrike thought. "Ain't nothin' but a Hound Dog . . ." reverberated in the cloistered, freezing outdoor air separating her from them; it pressed itself against the glass of her window. She flicked on the kitchen lights, opened her refrigerator, discovered she did have a bottle of beer, took it out, pried off the cap, raised the bottle's thick lip to her mouth and drank. The beer slid down her throat, taking several of her thoughts with it. She picked up her telephone and dialed Max. Busy.

A thread was hanging from the cuff of her shirt. It had once served a purpose and now served none. If one stitch could come undone, so could others. The thread struck her as both sad and threatening. She took her kitchen scissors from their drawer and snipped at it. But the scissors were dull, the thread slack. On her third try she succeeded. She picked up the thread from where it had fallen on the floor, rolled it between her fingers into a tiny, solid ball, a nearly weightless planet all its own, then dropped it in the garbage. An abrupt quiet filled the kitchen. No more Elvis. She looked out across the courtyard. The windows opposite were closed.

Yes, thought Ulrike in the sudden silence, I do remember the little wooden table that was mine, then Ingrid's. It was painted pale blue, and Gustave bought it from Dr. Lowen, a dentist who lived in our building, a man I disliked because whenever I saw him he asked me if I was enjoying my little table, and he asked in the tone adults use when inquiring if you've done something wrong. Beatrice, you ask what I know of your connection with my father. I know quite a bit. You say you want me to judge you. It is not possible for me to do so. I'm sorry that Ines is dead. This has nothing to do with me. What did Ines look like? I don't remember, not exactly. Her intensity I do remember, and her drawing also. She was drawing a map of the world, of her own invented world.

Ulrike swallowed another long throatful of beer, returned to the living room, took the bulky envelope from on top of her piano and sat down on the sofa.

You wonder how my father would describe me to you today, my father who's as dead as your daughter. Not that the death by cancer of a fifty-eight-year-old man and the death of an eighteen-year-old girl in a bicycle accident can be compared. Do you know how difficult your handwriting is to decipher? Your German, however, is excellent. I'm impressed. I should pack my clothes. You say I'm not obliged to read your letter, and you are right. I don't have to read it. But the fact remains that you've sent it.

Ulrike pulled the letter out. Every page was numbered and written for her. Not for her father, her mother or her sister, but for her. She's selected me, thought Ulrike. How will I describe my father to her? I'll tell her he's a man I adored. I'll tell her he's a man I detested. I can tell her whatever I please.

Ulrike found her place, and continued to read.

GUSTAVE ARRIVED in the long light of an afternoon. It was one of the last days of summer. My father put down the book he was reading and said, "That boat looks as though it's headed straight for us. Perhaps it's bringing Gustave Huguenot."

I came out on the front deck of our cottage and saw the white motorboat noisily cutting its way through the lake. My father stood up, folded his reading glasses. "Yes," my mother called from the screen porch. "It is coming to us." We started down the rocks.

Earlier in the summer I'd asked my father, "Who is Gustave Huguenot?"

My father had just come into the kitchen, reading aloud from a letter in which Gustave asked if he might visit us in late August. He would be attending a conference in Montreal. He would like to pass through Toronto and meet my father before returning to Berlin. Would my father be in Toronto? It would be an honour. He had heard, as a child, stories about my father. Gustave's mother, Claude, sent her warmest regards.

My father topped up his teacup. "Gustave Huguenot is the son of a wonderful fellow, an extraordinary man, Marcel Huguenot, whom I met in Switzerland just before the war and who, sadly, about seven years after the war, died of a heart attack. He wasn't yet forty-five when, just like that, he dropped dead in his own garden."

As my father wandered out of the kitchen, I followed him. He sat down in his chair, folded the letter and slipped it into the pocket of his dressing gown.

"Well?" I asked.

"In 1938, along with two university friends, I decided to explore Europe. We crossed over on a cattle boat. It was all a great adventure. Then, as we were cycling through Switzerland, I sprained my ankle. It was the sort of thing your awkward father was apt to do. I suggested to my two companions—Alf Greenbaum and Derek Fielding—that they go on, that I'd rest my ankle and catch up with them in a few weeks' time, in Strasbourg. It was a good thing I didn't play the hero and try to tough it out, because the weather turned foul. Those two, poor chaps, must have been wet as rats most days. They deserved better."

A cycling trip, Ulrike. My father balancing on a bicycle. I don't enjoy writing the word *bicycle.* Yet I could fill these pages with that one word. Bicycle. Bicycle. Bicycle. Bicycle.

—

My father continued his story:

"The hostel in Geneva, where I found a room for a reasonable price, was near a public library. I went to the library every day to read the paper. I felt quite pleased with myself for saving the price of a paper.

"Every afternoon a young man, the same young man, sat at the same table as I did. He looked to be about my age, perhaps a few years older. We fell into conversation. He'd recently arrived from France, he told me, along with his young wife, who'd been offered a research position in medicine at the University of Geneva.

"It was not often, then, that a man changed cities, let alone countries, for the sake of his wife's career. At any rate, I hadn't heard of any who had. This is no ordinary fellow, I told myself. I was curious to know what made him tick. His name was Marcel Huguenot, so he certainly wasn't a Catholic, which must have made him a bit of an outsider in France. He had a doctorate in physics.

"I should have been in Boston completing my own doctorate at that very moment, but I'd come up against a wall—that's why I'd fled for the summer. The entire field of linguistics, to which I'd given my energies for the past six years, struck me as pointless, an elaborate fiction, a rococo entertainment—nothing more. But I shouldn't be telling you this. It won't do you any good to know about your father's agonies. You'll have plenty of your own. All the same, it was unpleasant. When you can't go forward, or back.

"Four days after we met, Marcel found a fine position with a large glass manufacturing company. He came into the library to tell me. He said his only regret was that he wouldn't have time any more to sit about and read whatever he liked. I bought him a drink in a bar across the street. I used to know the name of that bar. It will come to me."

My father took a sip of his tea, unfolded his glasses, slipped them on, then unfolded the Saturday paper.

"Is that all?"

"I've got this paper to read."

"You can't just stop in the middle."

"But you've heard it all before."

"So what? You still haven't told me about Gustave Huguenot."

"Aha. So you're interested in him?"

"Not really. But if he's coming to visit us, I'd like to know who he is."

"I don't know much about him. I believe he teaches at the Free University in Berlin. He can't have been more than twelve when his father died. He was born during the war.

"The long and the short of it is that, when my ankle refused to heal, Marcel and his wife, Claude, most generously invited me to stay with them. Claude was too severe to be pretty, but she certainly wasn't plain. Her name seemed to me regrettable, but that was the fault of my pronunciation as much as anything. I wonder if it helped or hindered her to have such a masculine name in a masculine field?

"The harder I tried to think in French, the more German took over. German, for me, was safer ground. They spoke to each other in French and to me in German.

Claude treated me with a gracious reserve. Aha, I remember—The Gallant Boar—that was the name of the bar. Of course in German the joke wasn't half so good as it is in English. The Gallant Bore. What do guests and fish have in common? I'm sure you've heard this one? In any case, I must have left before I stank, because Marcel seemed keen to keep up a correspondence, and after the war, in 1951 to be precise, the year you were born, he and Claude turned up in Toronto for a day.

"Your mama and I had them to dinner—that is to say, your mother cooked them a splendid meal and I hung up their coats and talked at them while you, if I remember correctly, screamed your lungs out."

"Was Gustave with them?"

"No. They'd left him and his younger brother behind. Either Claude or Marcel had a conference to attend in New York. Was it Claude or Marcel? I don't remember. It was very good of them to stop over in Toronto."

Ulrike, did Gustave often tell you stories in which you figured as the culprit? I, according to my father, often "screamed my lungs out" as a baby and later made myself heard in equally unpleasant ways.

I expect Gustave did, occasionally, portray you in an unflattering light. But he would have done so in full consciousness. Gustave knew himself.

My own father's self-knowledge was less reliable. What my father understood of himself changed shape, like taffy, depending on which direction he pulled on it. When I was a child, he would cut off sticky wads of his identity and hand them to me. I adored my father.

It is morning. A few minutes ago, Isaac called upstairs to me from the front hall, to say that he was going out to buy this morning's paper.

Now he is standing on the sidewalk across the street from our house. I can see him from where I'm sitting. He has crouched down to tie the laces of his shoe. Though it is bitterly cold out, he's wearing neither boots, nor gloves, nor his hat. By the time I look up from writing this sentence, no doubt, he will have finished with his laces, and he will be disappearing up the street to buy a newspaper at the corner store.

No, he has not disappeared up the street. He's standing in the same spot as before, and for no apparent reason. Perhaps he's changed his mind about the paper, or he wants his gloves. Yes, he's crossing the street and coming straight toward our house. I expect his hands and feet are cold. I have difficulty believing that either he or I exist. But we do, and I can hear the front door opening.

Ulrike, to you I can speak. You live far away, and you don't really know me. Neither do I know you, though I mistakenly feel I do. When Ines was knocked from her bicycle, she was carrying in her knapsack something of mine that she'd taken without my knowledge—your father's letters to me, and mine to him.

She must have found them in my studio. Did she come

across them by chance, or because she was searching for them? I hadn't opened the box where I kept them in years. How old was Ines when she first read them? Did she take those letters to Montreal hoping to extract from them what I failed to give her? They handed me her knapsack and, when I opened it, there were Gustave's letters, and mine, neatly arranged by order of date. Arranged by Ines. She'd put them in a plastic folder to protect them and to keep them in order. She was riding with them on her back. Could she have saved herself if she'd not been preoccupied by those letters? No. The car came from behind, and too fast, too close. No degree of alertness on her part could have saved her. It didn't matter what she'd been reading. I told you that the gods, perhaps, took her life in order to punish me. But they can't have, because they don't exist. Her death was an accident, and therefore meaningless. Isn't meaninglessness the greatest form of punishment?

Isaac does not know what she was carrying. He'd left the hospital room and gone down the hall when I opened her knapsack, and by the time he returned I'd fit the plastic folder containing my letters and Gustave's into my shoulder bag. He does not know what I now have here, with me in my studio, what Ines was quite possibly engaged in reading just before she got on her bicycle and set out.

By the time I met Gustave, I knew all about his father, Marcel, and next to nothing about Gustave himself, except that he was Marcel's eldest son and a lecturer at a university in Berlin. Did he teach political science or some other subject? Neither of my parents could remember.

Gustave stepped onto our dock; a young man, twenty-eight years old, he stood in front of me, the round lenses of his glasses balanced on either side of his fine nose, and from behind the lenses his eyes looked at me. They were no colour in particular. They were surprisingly pale. Very well, they were hazel, but their expression made colour irrelevant.

His dark hair had already begun to retreat from his forehead; and as if to compensate for this show of pre-maturity or cowardice, his hair stuck out in wiry, defiant abundance from the sides and back of his head.

He was not tall but stood as if he were—slender and strong, his shoulders solid.

I didn't open my mouth. I stared without speaking, all my feelings backing up behind my tongue. I held out my hand, which he shook firmly.

He'd arrived. Now I could begin. I could face whatever lay ahead of me in life. Since childhood I'd imagined "him." In my dreams he was featureless, of no particular build or complexion. Yet a feeling of utter recognition swept through me. This was who and what I'd longed for, this man and the feeling of recognition he brought with him.

I sensed he was inhabited by everything I yearned to find in myself. I was mistaken. I would find out how different we were from each other. I was also correct. He did know how to open me.

Did I know what I felt at the time? Of course not. I couldn't have put it into words. You must laugh, Ulrike, if you like. There was sunlight on the water and a great white cloud behind the trees.

His lower lip was sensual, his upper lip austere. His eyes agreed with both lips. They laughed with pleasure and, in the same instant, scrutinized me. He smiled glee-fully. He glowed. Perhaps bales of stories were going up in flame inside him? Tales his father, Marcel Huguenot, had told him about my father? About me? No. It was unlikely he'd heard much about me. Marcel had died the year after I was born, Claude's career made heavy demands upon her. She wouldn't have spent time telling her teenaged son stories about Canadians.

Yet maybe recently, knowing Gustave was to travel to Canada, she'd said, "Is it in August you go? Your father's friend, the Canadian who sprained his ankle and stayed with us before the war, Eric Mann, you might look him up. He's a linguist at the university there; his wife's a librarian, very gracious. Their daughter must be how old? Let's see, we visited them in 1951, I think. You and Guillaume stayed with Tante Cecile. She spoiled you both, and you weren't eager to come home." I am guessing. We all invent more than we care to admit.

Gustave, whatever the stories he had or hadn't heard, knew the truth of me, every single one of my innermost thoughts, the moment he stepped onto our dock. That is what I believed. It is what I wanted to believe. I can see inside you, his eyes announced. May I explore?

"Hello," he said, balancing on the unsteady floating dock, and what did I answer?

"Hello."

"My God, you have your father's eyes and nose," my own father exclaimed, shaking Gustave's hand. "It's good of you to have come all this way. I hope the bus ride up from the city wasn't too dull? Not to mention the plane ride before that. How long were you in Montreal?"

"I'm so pleased to meet you," my mother slipped in.

"On the contrary, the pleasure is all mine. How generous of you to have invited me. These islands . . ."

I grabbed Gustave's suitcase and ran. He reached out to stop me from taking his luggage, but he wasn't quick enough. I fled up the rocks. Behind me, I could hear my father laughing, saying loudly, "Well, there's not much point the rest of us staying down here."

But Gustave's voice had sowed its seed in my ear. His voice was growing in my ear as I climbed the rocks. It was filling me with his intonations. I looked over my shoulder and saw him with my parents, climbing. The motorboat was disappearing behind the next island out, the roar of its engine trailing behind, making the air ragged.

They'd nearly caught up with me. I reached the porch steps, climbed them and sat down. Gustave's suitcase beside me, I waited.

Gustave stopped beside the juniper bush at the top of the rock slope. He was alone. My parents must have been someplace, but I don't remember where. The bush was covered with small waxy berries that I knew smelled of gin when I dug my fingernails into them, then crushed them between my fingers. Had this man ever crushed juniper berries between his fingernails?

He looked up at me, where I sat with his suitcase at my side.

"Do I strike you as so weak?" he asked, amused.

"No."

Not for a moment did he think I'd taken his suitcase to relieve him of its weight. Yet there was a hint of anxiety behind his amusement. My opinion of him mattered to him. His vulnerability pleased me. It was not overwhelming. Just enough.

"Do you always carry men's suitcases for them?"

"No."

"Then I should feel honoured?"

"Yes."

"I am honoured."

"Yes. You are."

I got up and walked into the house, leaving his suitcase on the front porch. To occupy my hands, I filled the kettle with water from the pail beneath the counter and lit the stove.

Do you know how old I am? I am fifty-one and telling you a story I've no right to tell you; I've no right, not because you are Gustave's daughter but because Ines is dead and no more stories are possible. However, I must continue with this one. Perhaps I don't want you to judge me. Perhaps I want only to escape, just as I wanted to do back then. But you mustn't allow me to escape.

What did my "love affair" with your father consist of? Letters. Not only letters. But letters. They went on for pages, tiny footnotes climbing along the edges, weaving in and out of what was written five minutes before. I used whatever paper came to hand.

He wrote his best letters on postcards—a dozen in a single envelope, each picture a comment on the text.

As she rode down l'avenue du Parc, what thoughts were in Ines' mind? I could so easily have burned those letters and postcards, had I known what was to come. How long did she have them in her possession? What does any of this matter now? When I dropped her off at Union Station, where she was to catch the train for Montreal, I got out of our car and stood beside her on the sidewalk. She glanced at her watch, then gave me a searching look followed by a quick, brilliant smile. I offered to carry one of her bags, reminding her that she already had the weight of her knapsack on her back. She looked away from me at the mention of her knapsack. I assumed it was the quantity of what she was carrying that embarrassed her. I had no inkling she had taken something that was mine. She kissed me, allowed me to hug her, picked up her bags and hurried off.

—

I am going downstairs now. Isaac won't be there. He won't suggest that I eat something or that I get some fresh air, because he isn't home. He's gone to the movies.

At first we didn't write, Gustave and I. I was over thirty by the time we started corresponding. Gustave said that a letter was worth more than a conversation.

He wore a watch with a green leather strap when he came to Toronto to visit me. By then I was thirty-nine and living with Isaac. I was the mother of a child. I was Ines' mother. He arrived on a Wednesday and left the next day. On the day after he left, I walked about my city, the image of Gustave's wrist, with his watch strapped to it, hanging in front of my eyes. I forced myself to see, instead of his wrist and green watch strap, the delicate spring leaves growing on the bushes, to study the colour and texture of the bricks behind the bushes. I spoke his name, testing to see which was more real—his name or the bushes and bricks.

The moment his name formed in my mind, the rest of my body behaved as if he were about to come around the corner, as if he were about to walk up to me and take off my clothes, to free me of everything unnecessary. My breasts grew heavy and just below my belly I opened to receive him.

Am I sorry, Ulrike, to be imposing upon you this description of the desire I once felt for your father? It's not much of a description.

He was not coming around the corner. I stood rooted to the sidewalk, stunned as a night animal, caught in the glare of an incomprehensible truth: he was across the Atlantic Ocean. He was elsewhere, and I had no idea when I would see him again. I wanted to step out of the way of the truth, but couldn't. His absence rolled through me.

Ines' absence I am refusing. It is too large. Its proportions won't allow it to be given a shape. I can neither pick it up nor put it down. I can't climb over it. I want to crawl inside it but mustn't.

I've jumped far ahead. A moment ago I was seventeen and standing on my parents' dock. Gustave stepped out of a white motorboat, a suitcase in his hand. "Hello," we both said, "hello." Was I transformed on the spot, liberated? Not immediately, certainly not. But a window opened and, for several days, air rushed in. Also images and ideas: a dreary courtyard in Berlin, where an aged landlady sat on a folding chair reading the paper to a tenant as old as herself and going blind; a rose, a bicycle stand; a brief summary of the significance of the Frankfurt School of Marxist philosophy; Gustave's naked foot, my uneven breasts inside my bathing suit, my wide hips, the disturbing clump of hairs growing from your father's right shoulder blade, my spine—all of these tumbled in through the window.

Gustave planned to stay for two days. Much of the time my father laid claim to him, leading him off into the woods to admire a particular tree, to discuss the evolution of German grammar, the student revolts in Berlin, anti-American sentiment, the airlift that saved Berlin between '48 and '49, the wall now dividing the city in two. At the dinner table, though my mother and I threw in a few questions, my father, omnipotent linguist, directed the course of all conversation. Ours was an old-fashioned household.

The afternoon of Gustave's last day with us, he and I lingered on the long smooth rocks that formed the front tip of the island. My parents had gone up to change out of their bathing suits. There was no breeze and the lake lay without a murmur. The crazed gnawing of a chainsaw leapt from the mainland but died away abruptly.

I wrapped my arms around my knees and asked your father to describe the apartment where he lived in Berlin. I requested every detail. Once I held a clear picture of the courtyard, stairwell, green bathroom to the right as you entered the apartment itself, living-room wall lined with bookshelves from ceiling to floor, narrow grey kitchen, red chair in his study, I asked, "What do you really teach?"

"Not what interests me most."

"What interests you most?"

He listed Adorno, Horkheimer, Habermas, three names unknown to me at the time. As he attempted to explain each thinker, his excitement grew, then he studied my face. "No. It is too difficult," he said. "It's taken me years, and I understand only a part of what they're saying. May I try again?"

"Of course."

Your father's desire to acquaint me with the beauty of these minds that he so admired hummed in the heat of the afternoon; it vibrated in the still air. What was revealed to me was his own beauty.

From his careful explanations I retained only a title: *Knowledge and Human Interests.* I suspected that Marxism would never lastingly excite me, however engaged I was in that moment by your father's enthusiasm. I distrusted theories.

"Any theory is a thread, dangling in a salt solution," I announced.

I could suddenly see the short bit of string I'd tied to the middle of a pencil in grade school, how it had hung in the water and become miraculously encrusted in salt. I felt certain all theories attracted formations of seemingly solid facts, whereas the truth existed always as a liquid.

"Is that so?" your father asked.

"Yes. Beautiful crystals form, but they're not really solid, not in an enduring way. Toss them back in the water, they dissolve."

"But the thread is insoluble?" His laughter twitched at the corner of his mouth.

"Perhaps."

"And according to you I spend my days dipping my nose in a mental salt solution. Perhaps crystals have formed on the tip of my nose?"

"I don't see any. Tell me about Berlin. Is Berlin beautiful?"

"In Berlin we drink lots of beer. Do you like to drink beer?"

"Sometimes."

"Not much?"

"Beer's not necessary."

His laughter broke free, but immediately he straightened his spine and tried to draw his laughter back inside himself. He fixed his serious eyes on me. He sat stiffly, a sentinel guarding my feelings, quite determined not to hurt me with his amusement.

"Is Berlin beautiful?" I asked again.

"Not at all."

He described the dreary buildings, the slabs of concrete and glass being thrown together at great expense, the West's failing attempt to make a showpiece of its half-a-city. "It's no longer a true capital. No quantity of Deutschmarks can save it from provincialism or make it less claustrophobic.

"It's an invalid being fed by intravenous. What sort of 'cultural centre' relies on swallowing capsules of creativity brought in from elsewhere? Art can't be forced into existence. Writers pass through Berlin, but they don't stay. No one stays. Yes, quite a few painters are making Berlin their home, but most of them are mediocre. They stay because they'd rather be big in a pond than puny in an ocean. Music is the exception. In music there's a real striving for excellence. But the universities are in chaos."

"Why do you stay?"

He picked up a loose stone and passed it back and forth between his hands.

"I like living on a fault line. There is so much in Berlin that is unresolved, buried just inches down. The atrocities of the past. The hopeless hope of reunification, the fear of never uniting."

With the stone in his hand he started to scratch distractedly at the rock we were sitting on. Then he noticed what he was doing and tossed the stone into the lake. I'd been hoping to keep it, as a sacred object, something that had rested in his palm. He picked up another stone and began to play with it.

"Just when I think, 'This is too claustrophobic and tedious to bear, this city has finally given up its ideals and fallen asleep, or worse—this false metropolis has never had any true ideals,' then the curious spirit of the place hits me. I walk home, juggling all sorts of possibilities in my imagination, quite drunk on a future Berlin that may never come into being."

He reached over his shoulder and scratched his back. His skin slid across his ribs just as mine would do if I were to raise my arm and scratch my back. I studied his ribs as he lowered his arm.

"It's a city as full of contradictions as I am, as cowardly. I didn't dare choose Paris. Most of my friends who didn't stay in Switzerland headed off to conquer Paris. I had a grandmother there. I spoke French. My mother was born there, and my father in Calais. Instead I chose Berlin, a city as cut off and confused as myself."

He smiled at me, confident in his confusion.

"You're confused?"

"How could I not be?"

I waited for him to say more. He pulled out a pack of cigarettes from the pocket of his shirt, which lay beside him.

"And you, Beatrice, you will be studying linguistics when you start university in the fall?"

"I suppose so."

"You don't want to?"

"It's not what matters most to me."

"What matters most to you?"

The afternoon shade had not yet reached the point where we sat. A punishing heat beat on my head; for an eternity the sun had been searing my arms and legs. Rather than answer him I dove into the lake.

I swam. I stopped and looked back. He gave no sign of getting up. He was smoking his cigarette and watching me. I waved and he waved back. I swam farther, keeping close to the shore so that I'd not find myself in the path of a boat, and so that I could watch the trees glide past, one by one.

Ulrike, every stroke pulled me through my conversation with your father. I swam through his living room, past the bookshelves, through the grey kitchen, the green bathroom, onward into the demanding thoughts of Jürgen Habermas, which were tangled and slippery, largely incomprehensible, disturbing as duckweed. Then I looked up at the shore.

The trees were more beautiful than before, made sharper, clearer by the tug of the conversation pulling me away from them. One day I'd swim off into a vast, bottomless conversation.

A birch tree leaned over the water. I floated beneath it, so close I could see each curl of bark pulling away from the trunk.

Yes, Ulrike, a birch tree will always be virginal, spare and graceful, bone white. Romance won't be killed off. Have my descriptions of your father made you uncomfortable? Have you recognized him?

Gustave reached inside me and pulled something out, as if I were a hat. What did he pull out? A rabbit? Silk scarves? It was me he pulled out. I stared at myself. Then he slipped me quickly back inside. Was it all a trick? Or had he performed some sort of magic?

A birch tree is untouchable. Her white negates the surrounding woods. But in the very act of swallowing her surroundings, she amplifies them, makes them darker, richer. A birch tree gobbles but appears pure. She devours more deviously than a black hole.

What do you think? Was it Gustave I was in love with?

And what of Ines? Did I love or consume her? Mothers so often attempt to devour their daughters. As a young child, Ines detested being kissed, but I could not stop myself. How lovely her soft cheek felt against my lips. The year she turned twelve, she asked me for a violin and lessons. I convinced Isaac, not without considerable effort, that a violin would be too difficult and expensive an instrument. We bought her, at my suggestion, a guitar, and for two years Ines dutifully attended her lessons. I praised her indifferent progress until she screwed up her courage to ask, burdened with guilt, and beneath her guilt furious, if she might abandon the instrument she said we'd so generously given her. "Yes," I told myself, "I was right not to get her a violin. She has no real interest in music. Why would she? I myself have no musical ability. And yet it's a shame she's giving up. She was learning to play her guitar quite prettily."

It is relatively easy to say "I love you" and difficult to allow those closest to us to be themselves. Did I try to swallow Ines, to consume her? Whatever shoes Ines chose, I either disapproved of them or coveted them. On two occasions I tried to find a similar pair for myself.

In the hot late afternoon, while Gustave lay on the point, I swam along the shore toward the opposite end of the island. The pines held the light in their long arms. They whispered their refreshing indifference, soft needles swaying in the highest, coolest air. A squat oak stood in the still heat. I turned and swam back. I'd suddenly realized it wasn't the trees I was about to lose but Gustave. I swam as quickly as I could. He was there, he'd not gone up to the cottage; he was lying on his back, his sun hat covering his face.

I climbed out of the water, crouched a foot away from him. However hard I stared at his hat, it didn't move. Was he sleeping? I leaned a few inches forward and looked straight down at his stomach, at the knot in his centre that would never be untied.

A path of dark hairs led away from his navel, toward his chest. A second path led down, and disappeared under the waistband of the turquoise swimming trunks that hid his genitals. I couldn't make out their exact shape, not with my eyes. My fingers could have told me more. Or my mouth? The odd-shaped, uneven mound pressed against the turquoise cloth.

My hand? Was it mine? My mouth? Both were mine, and the desire to touch him also mine. How could my own hand frighten me? My mouth scare me?

His foot moved. My gaze sailed down his thighs, over his knees and down his shins to his once-more-immobile foot. The fragility of his ankles reminded me that he'd once been a child.

Without warning, he removed his hat. My eyes travelled so rapidly up his body toward the movement of his hat, there was no time to send my attention off in the direction of the lake. My eyes met his. I stumbled into the middle of his eyes, into their look of tender amusement.

As he sat up, his expression sobered.

"You didn't answer my question. Unless you meant me to understand that swimming is what matters to you the most?"

"Sculpture."

"Sculpture matters most?"

"Yes," I answered quickly. Did he know of the desire hiding in my hand and mouth? Yes. He knew. He'd felt my eyes consume his skin. Besides, he could see inside my head.

"What will you study in the fall?"

"Linguistics."

"Oh yes?"

"Mediocrity in anything is awful. But it is the most awful in a work of art."

I hardly knew what I was saying. He'd felt how close I'd come to touching him.

"Possibly," he answered.

"Don't you agree?"

"For you it is. For me also. Beyond that it is more complicated."

"In any case, what I would produce as a sculptor would most certainly be mediocre."

"Most certainly?"

"A true artist knows from a young age. There are signs. I show no signs."

"None at all?"

"Not of brilliance."

"Who says brilliance cannot be achieved through hard work? And if not brilliance, then admirable quality?"

"My father. He'd agree about admirable quality. But brilliance can't be achieved."

"And so, if there are no signs of certain brilliance?"

"Then it would be self-indulgent to insist, to promote an illusion. It would be pursuing a lie."

"And what does your mother say?"

"That I show plenty of signs of brilliance. But what she says doesn't matter."

"Why?"

"Because."

"What would she have to do to make her opinions matter?"

He saw I had no answer. He pushed at a loose stone with his foot. When he'd done thinking, he looked at me.

"I understand your fear, or a part of it. I wanted to study philosophy but didn't dare to. I knew that my mediocrity would disgust me. I chose political science because it matters less to me."

I shifted my gaze from my toes to the water. Far down there, clams were dragging themselves, each digging a faint trail in the sand. Was Gustave's honesty a form of courage? Did this confession of his compensate for his failure to have chosen courageously?

"Couldn't you change to philosophy?"

"Not now." He laughed.

I was seventeen. My determination to believe that anything could be undone perhaps appealed to him.

"No," he said. "It's too late. I must stick with political science. It's what I'm capable of. Just as Berlin, provincial, divided, with its troubling past, is the city that suits me best."

"Then you're doing something terrible to your life," I exclaimed.

"Is that what you think?" he asked. "I could have betrayed myself in far worse ways."

He stood up, reached down for his towel and flipped it over his shoulder. "Let's go up. The sun is gone."

I'd offended him.

—

That evening at dinner, my mother invited Gustave to stay a few days longer.

"But I've already imposed."

"Hogwash," my father proclaimed. "Do you know how long your poor parents put up with me? Besides, you're a fine fellow, and we're enjoying your company immensely, or I certainly am."

"We all are," said my mother.

I cut the chicken on my plate into the finest slices possible.

"Well," he said after a moment's silence. "My flight leaves on Friday, and I'd thought I would spend a while in Toronto, but I'd rather be here. So, I accept and thank you. I'd be delighted to stay until Thursday."

Two more days. I looked up. He was waiting for me to look up.

What an arrogant, foolish thought. Who wouldn't choose a breezy, pine-scented island over the streets of a city in the last days of summer?

He stared straight into my eyes. No, it was not the island. I was the reason for his staying. Where was the arrogance in recognizing what was true?

All the next day I waited for some gesture of proof. I craved more solid evidence.

Ulrike, do you demand proof from your lovers? Are you as guilty as I am of lack of faith? Guilty of impatience, guilty of greed? Guilty of being human? Is your guilt a revolving door? Once it releases you, do you rush back in? This time I do not want my guilt to release me.

It is one in the morning. Isaac is sitting in some bar on Queen Street, drinking beer. I don't expect he'll come home drunk. I've never seen him seriously drunk, and possibly he now feels, as I do, that his own capacity for self-destruction is watching him like an owl, and that he must be very careful.

But I do not know what he is thinking or feeling. He suggested I go with him to Queen Street and I declined, and he didn't insist. I caught up with him on the stairs and kissed him on the back of his neck. He turned, gave me a quizzical look and said, "I won't stay out late."

But he has always tended to stay up later than I do. I expect he will be home soon. Though "home" no longer describes this house.

Our cottage on our island, my parents' and mine, was, as I've told you, a large tent made of wood. On the exposed girders, jars of nails, playing cards, cups filled with pencils, candle stubs, selected stones accumulated.

Your father's last night on the island, I lit a fire in the stove with the two iron doors that swung open and folded out of the way. I lit the row of candles and the propane lamp we used to see by, and we played charades. My mother became a silent Billie Holiday. My father, leaping about in lederhosen then whipping invisible cream, revealed his true identity—that of a dessert, a Bavarian cream.

Gustave pulled the words "Dominion of Canada" from the hat on the table. He mimed a dome, arms above his head, and then sliced an onion, while weeping copious, fictitious tears.

We ran out of words and listened to the moths beat their fine dry wings against our bright windows. We listened to their demand that we allow them to perish in the flames of the candles on our table. But we refused to let them in.

My daughter, Ines, died just as she was beginning her second year studying classics at McGill University. She died exactly three months and three weeks ago today. On September 25, in the afternoon, she rode her bicycle, as I've told you, down l'avenue du Parc. She always wore her helmet, but on this particular afternoon she went bareheaded.

When she was a child, and also as a teenager, she used to try to convince me to wear my helmet, and occasionally I listened to her. But I detested feeling confined.

I felt protected. By my faith in what? I couldn't say. My mind scoffed at any form of faith, while my heart insisted that I was safe. Hadn't I ridden for years without a helmet and survived? A helmet diminished my pleasure.

Ines wore her helmet always, without fail. Then one day she did not wear her helmet. How far does my guilt extend? What sort of woman would ride without a helmet, for years, knowing she was setting a poor example for her daughter?

A selfish one? A negligent, self-absorbed, stupid, unforgivable one? If I chastise myself sufficiently, will Ines come back? If I refuse to leave this room, if I keep writing forever, will she return?

The moths beat their wings against our thin glass windows. We sat in the candlelight and listened to them. Gustave, my parents and I. The flames burned and the moths beat.

Ulrike, who can I ask to forgive me?

Isaac cannot do so because he does not consider me guilty of Ines' death. I have not told him that she was carrying my letters on her back. As for the question of her helmet, yesterday he said to me, with justifiable harshness, "Ines knew your refusal to wear a helmet was stupid and irresponsible. She said so repeatedly. She had my example. I wore mine and she wore hers. She was proud of wearing hers. Then one day she didn't. Why was she bareheaded that particular day? Who knows? We'll never know. But I don't believe she was finally following your example, or trying to prove anything to you. Maybe she was in a hurry or she'd forgotten her helmet somewhere. Who knows? It wasn't because of you, Beatrice. That's all we know. That's it. It wasn't because of you. Why do you go on and on?"

I am guilty of going on and on. He sounds weary. Ines' death has exhausted him, and I add to his exhaustion. He assures me I did not fail Ines, and for an hour or more I choose to believe him. The letters become an unanswerable question. He's right. No one knows why she was riding bare-headed. For an hour I am not guilty, he has forgiven me. Then I remember he does not know what she'd been reading, I realize I am guilty of having deceived him long ago, I remember that Ines is still dead, and that he must not forgive me.

Ulrike, all those letters I sent to your father. You must have seen them arrive. Did you wonder about them? Did they hurt you? And your mother? I expect they hurt your mother.

Your father's last night with us, the moon climbed, immense behind the islands. The sky was clear; stars fell into the black, unblinking lake. The moon floated higher. Soon it would also plunge into the lake. I came down the rocks and saw him where I'd thought he might be.

He was sitting at the water's edge, smoking a cigarette. I started to slide the canoe into the lake. "May I help?" he asked, standing up.

"No, thank you."

I stepped into the stern of the boat and settled myself, willing him to ask if he might come along.

"Is there room for a second person?" he asked.

"Of course."

He stubbed out his cigarette, then climbed lightly in at the bow.

We paddled toward the far end of the bay, keeping close to the shore of the island, peering now and then into the obscurity of the woods, holding our paddles still, listening for any movement. At the side of the canoe, stars floated, brilliant promises of release. Suddenly, your father spoke.

"Soon you'll be attending classes, making new friends, meeting lots of young men."

"Will I? I hope the courses won't be too dull."

Did he really believe that young men might show an interest in me? I couldn't search his face for an answer. He'd spoken with his back to me, no doubt concerned that to turn might mean tipping the canoe. "Why are you fated to be confused?" I asked.

"Am I?"

"You said so, the other day on the point, you said you couldn't help but be confused."

"You're right," he admitted, and now he risked turning to glance at me. "You have a good memory."

"Well?"

"My mother's a Jew who, quite by chance, left France for Switzerland just before the war. She did not consider herself Jewish." He took up his paddle again. "My grandmother remained in France. My mother wrote to her to say she must leave Paris immediately.

"My grandmother wouldn't hear of it. My mother argued with her by mail. My grandmother refused to believe she was in any danger. She'd escaped the provincial tedium of Smolensk when she was sixteen by marrying a colleague of her father's, whom she promptly divorced upon arriving in Paris. Paris was hers. She had no intention of ever leaving Paris.

"My grandmother; her behaviour in 1906 had been highly unusual for a young woman. Divorced and free, she'd enrolled at the Sorbonne in the faculty of law."

"You're confused because of your grandmother? It's her fault?"

"You're right again." He laughed. "It's not her fault. At twenty-eight I'm responsible for my own confusion. But my grandmother is interesting, don't you think? Or am I boring you?"

"No, you're not. But I'd rather hear about you."

"About me? You'd soon discover how much more interesting my grandmother is. I'll tell you about my grandmother, and afterwards you can tell me about yours."

"If I want to."

"Yes. If you want to. I won't force you to do anything you don't want to do. I'm very polite. I was raised to be polite."

"How admirable."

I couldn't tell from the tone of his voice if he was mocking me or nervous. Was it possible I could be unnerving a grown man?

He stopped paddling and asked, "May I stop paddling for a moment?"

"Of course."

He rubbed the back of his neck. Silence spread around us, lay under and above us; darkness also.

"Tell me about your grandmother," I requested.

"Ah, you see. So, my grandmother." He slipped his

paddle back into the water and pulled. "Every day my mother, pushing me in my stroller, changing my diaper, nursing me, imagined she would receive, that very day, the news that my grandmother had been rounded up, taken away. But such news never came.

"My grandmother survived the occupation. The war ended. My mother took my brother and me to meet our grandmother. But I didn't fall in love with Paris.

"Of my grandmother's relatives in Poland, all had been killed, of her Russian siblings, cousins and aunts, a few remained. My grandmother refused to speak of those who had not survived. Murder, said my mother.

"Every morning my grandmother sat at her desk and wrote for two hours, then moved to her sofa, where she remained until noon, rereading the works of Montaigne. Most mornings my mother kept my brother and me out of the apartment.

"A thick biography of Napoleon lay on my grand-mother's bedside table. 'Are we Jews?' my mother demanded. I've never once set foot in a synagogue.

"I sat on my grandmother's balcony overlooking the Seine and read about Berlin. By then I must have been fourteen or fifteen. My father had died. We spent two weeks of every summer in Paris. Everyone was speaking of Bertolt Brecht. In East Berlin, the Russians had given him a theatre of his own.

"A family who lived in the apartment below my grand-mother's, and who had a son my age, invited me to go with them to see *The Caucasian Chalk Circle*. After that, I dreamed of travelling to East Germany, of seeing *Mother Courage and Her Children,* directed by the master himself. Then, without warning, Brecht died. My interest in Berlin only grew more intense."

"And your confusion? That was then. What about now?"

"In this canoe?"

The tenderness in his voice frightened me.

"No," I said. "In Berlin."

He straightened his back and answered my question. "I'm a Swiss half-Jew, of French and Russian extraction, living in a German city that is divided in two. I spend my days in a small room, reading the efforts of innumerable political theorists, searching for threads of ideas to twist into a rope upon which society might, balancing carefully above the abyss, take a few steps toward justice. Does that answer your question?"

"A little."

"That's already something. Now, are you going to tell me about your grandmother?"

What did I tell him? I don't remember.

On the granite point of my parents' island, we lifted out the canoe and turned it over. He'd spoken of the Holocaust. I pictured his grandmother, the yellow star sewn to the breast of her coat. It was as if he'd rung a huge bell that made no sound, that released a dense silence.

Is that why I didn't touch the back of his hand as we stood beside the canoe? I wanted fiercely to act, to feel his skin where it stretched over his knuckles, to press down on the bluish vein that crossed the back of his hand. His hand rubbed his cheek then dropped to hang inches from my own in the night air.

He was a man touched by History. In 1956, while I'd played in my parents' Toronto backyard, he'd perched on a Paris balcony, reading the announcement of Brecht's death in *Le Monde.* Yet here dangled his hand, separated from mine by an inch or two of darkness.

As we climbed the rocks toward the lighted cottage, Gustave stopped abruptly. I stopped also and looked at him. He studied my face for a moment, then concluded, "You're beautiful."

"You think so because it's dark out," I said and walked quickly on ahead.

The following morning your father left, and two weeks later I enrolled at the University of Toronto, where for the next four years I studied linguistics and told myself that sculpture, for me, would have been a senseless self-indulgence.

Isaac has just parked our car in front of our house. He is lucky to have found a spot. Even at two in the morning it is not always easy to find parking on our street, though we all pay for a permit. He is not getting out of the car. I expect he is listening to the radio. There, he's turned off the engine and the headlights, and now he is climbing out.

Ulrike studied the round face of her watch. Beneath the glass the second hand jerked methodically forward, climbing, while the minute and hour hands waited. I must pack, she thought, and setting aside the pages she'd read she got up from the sofa.

She took two dresses from her closet and laid them on her bed. One was raw silk, the blue of distances at dusk. It was simple, and hung well on her small, wiry body, which she'd inherited for the most part from her father. She was fond of the blue dress. Its square neckline revealed her collarbone. The second dress was black, of a softer material that fit tightly, drawing attention to her slender hips, and to her breasts. She was equally fond of the black dress.

She lifted down her suitcase from the closet shelf and set it on her bed. She opened it.

Do you want to know why Ines borrowed or stole your correspondence with my father? Curiosity. She wanted to read those letters, and to see how you'd react to her theft. She wanted to provoke you. Or she believed that luck would allow her to return everything, unnoticed, to its proper place. And then a car swerved.

You don't believe in punishing gods any more than I do. I'm glad you admit this. But what you want to believe is another matter. You want to feel guilty rather than truly suffer. You hope your guilt will be forgiven and you'll experience relief. I'd also like to be forgiven. By whom and for what, I'm not sure.

Ulrike pulled open the top drawer of her dresser, in which her underpants were folded neatly. They weren't, however, in their proper place. They were relegated to the far left, where her socks belonged. Her socks had vanished. She moved her bras aside. Aha. She'd found her socks, and three were missing their mates. Her pantyhose lay undisturbed. Max. She smiled. This was the work of Max. When he'd come by yesterday, she'd felt she was losing her mind while practising, suddenly unable to do justice to the *Goldberg Variations*, to find in herself the calm clarity she yearned for and that the variations required of her. Max, to appease her, had done the laundry.

She trusted Max, but not certain feelings he evoked in her, an unspeakable desire to give in, the sensation that her anger, the undirected fury she'd felt much of her life, was not an inalienable part of her. Max did not feel responsible for the world in the vast, ill-defined way that she did. He had, therefore, less reason to shut the world out. He possessed a looseness, a contortionist's ability to extricate himself from tense social situations. She both admired his flexibility and considered it suspect. He could pick open a lock using a wire. She'd seen him do it, when he'd locked his keys in his car. She couldn't accuse him of lacking discipline. He played his cello beautifully. Yet he avoided playing as a soloist. His reluctance to advance his career irritated her. A form of blind confidence allowed him to shoot along the autobahn with one hand on the wheel, or to talk on his cellphone while cycling through traffic. She adored the shape of his feet.

Ulrike took four pairs of underpants and set them in a corner of her suitcase. The telephone rang.

"Hello?"

"Hello," said Max. "Shall I come over?"

"I thought you were busy."

"I thought so too, but I'm not. The rehearsal was cancelled."

"Good. I'd like to get out of this place. How soon can you be here? We'll go out."

"Have you eaten?"

"No."

"Neither have I."

"How soon will you get here?"

"An hour. An hour and a half?"

"Wonderful."

They hung up their respective telephones. Easy, she thought. Life can be easy.

She chose earrings, a necklace, shirts and pants, fit these and everything else she'd need into her suitcase, which she closed and set on the floor. Immediately, several sentences from Beatrice's letter lit up in her mind like heat lightning— "We all invent more than we care to admit. I envied your father's watch strap. Your mother was dressed all in white." The words vanished as quickly as they'd appeared, and in their place stood her father, in front of the stone house where she'd spent her childhood summers, high in the Alps. He was clearing his throat of phlegm while tugging on his earlobe, in imitation of the baker from the village below. Next he performed the baker's wife, gossiping with a customer.

Ulrike fished in her pocket for her lip balm. We all invent more than we care to admit. She unscrewed the lid of the round container and rubbed some balm on her lips.

What exactly is it that you want from me, Beatrice? I invented you, when I was fourteen. Not your appearance. I knew what you looked like, that your hands were large and bony, that you had long legs, small breasts and a rather wide mouth. I'd seen you in my parents' living room. But your emotions, your beliefs I invented. I wanted my younger sister, Ingrid, to join in, to help me in my project. But she refused. She was completely unwilling to speculate about your letters. I couldn't figure out if she thought your relationship with Gustave was innocent, or a silly adult game that was beneath her consideration. I suspected it frightened her. But she showed no fear. Ingrid rarely admitted to being frightened by anything. I was not Ingrid, nor am I Ingrid now, and I am the one you've chosen to write to. Why? Because of something Gustave told you about me?

A green watch strap. You may be right. My father may have worn a green watch strap. He had more than one watch. He liked to have more. More neckties, more chocolates, more admiration. For such a dry, severe man, he was surprisingly greedy. My father, whose name you found sexually arousing. You claim that placing his name in your mouth, shaping it with your tongue, made your breasts grow heavy. All right, you didn't put it in quite those terms, but nearly. You apologize to me for describing your desire. Then you go right on describing it. And you've guessed correctly. I am eager to know about my father. Now that he's dead, every last detail interests me. Though I'm not sure I appreciate your making me aware of how curious I feel about his private life. What uncomfortable truth shall I face you with? Is that the idea? You imagine that if you offend me sufficiently, I'll become angry, and do what? Phone you and scream, "Ines is dead," keep screaming the truth at you until you listen? Maybe you will anger me to that point, but for now I mostly pity you. I pity you but am willing to confess that some of your questions intrigue me. Do I demand proof from my lovers? Yes, I do. I am demanding. You seem to know me quite well.

Ulrike picked up her suitcase, carried it into the living room and set it down beside her music bag. I'm surprised your husband, Isaac, isn't packing his suitcases right now.

Beatrice's letter lay waiting for her on the sofa.

ULRIKE, I AM PRACTISED at closing my studio door. I have learned to be good at it. A woman must be on her guard. We believe we control the tides inside everyone, but we are not the moon. We must be willing to shut out our husbands, our lovers, brutally, in order to think and work, or simply to sit alone.

This morning, I made myself a cup of coffee, came straight in here and closed the door. Only then did I hesitate for a moment. It was the action of closing my door. I felt, irrationally, that I'd shut out Ines. I forced myself not to get up and open the door. I sat and listened for any movement in the downstairs hall, or on the stairs, any breath or rustling different from Isaac's, any sounds other than my own in this studio. Was I expecting a ghost? Hoping for one? I was listening out of habit deeper than habit.

Within moments of her birth, Ines took possession of my ear. First she filled it with small grunting, nuzzling noises. Her mouth and nose advanced urgently toward the milk-smell of my breast. From then on my ear followed her, gathering up every sound she dropped.

As she grew and spent more time out of my ear's reach, my ear slowly accepted her absence. It experienced a certain relief. I filled it with my own thoughts, with music and conversation. My ear suffered moments of panic. What if it were never to hear Ines make another sound?

Now my ear is listening again, and intently, for the rustlings or the voice of someone whose age is impossible to know. Is my daughter eighteen or five? Both at once?

My ear sorts through its inventory of her noises: the crumpling of a paper, her tapping foot, a hummed tune, a night cough, a conversation with a doll, curses directed at a computer, the pages of an essay being torn in half.

Gustave once told me that his Aunt Cecile believed in angels. Did he speak to you much about his Aunt Cecile? He didn't share his aunt's belief. But it was her gentleness and generosity that had saved him as a child, he claimed, and therefore he wished he could believe in angels, as she did. Never mind.

Angels. Ines' imagination accepted them, but her sense of logic refused them. When she was eight she told me she wanted to believe that her grandfather, my father, was floating about, watching us, but that she knew he wasn't. "Once we're dead there's nothing," she said in a tone of mild disappointment.

"Are you sure?" I asked.

"It's not what I want to think," she explained. "But I know. I know that's how it is."

—

You've met Isaac, but I doubt you remember him. That evening on Nürnberger Strasse was the evening that changed everything, or so I thought for a long time.

I wanted to escape from living an imperfect life. I was greedy. I yearned to be released from life's slow, murky current, to be freed into clarity by a rushing passion. I hoped for a momentous change.

And now, everything is changed. Ines is gone. Is this my clarity?

I was cutting the meat on my plate, that evening on Nürnberger Strasse. What sort was it? I was a vegetarian and eating it only out of politeness. The meat tasted unpleasant, and I concentrated on the potatoes, which were scalloped and delicious. Your mother, Gerda, had gone to such trouble. She'd arranged the asparagus beautifully on an blue oval serving plate.

"Isaac, Isaac," said Gustave, and he smiled an admiring smile at my husband. "When I first met Beatrice, on her parents' island, I tried hard to capture her attention but failed. She evaded all my overtures." He was speaking loudly. We'd all drunk quite a bit of wine. He swept his hand through the air to illustrate my evasion. From my end of the table I tried to touch his eyes with mine, but he got up to open another bottle.

He'd been speaking in German. I don't think he was aware how little Isaac understood of what he'd said, and he didn't appear to care what Gerda heard. He sat down again, looked straight at me and asked, "Do you remember?" What could I answer?

And you, Ulrike, what do you remember? I suggested, a moment ago, that Isaac was unlikely to have made a lasting impression on you. You hardly saw him. While we adults sat down to dinner, your sister vanished and you stayed, generously, in the living room, to keep Ines company. Every once in a while we heard the two of you laughing wildly. You didn't speak the same language. What were you doing in there? When I asked Ines, she said, "Having fun."

"What is Ulrike like?" I asked.

"I don't know her very well. But I like her."

Later I wrote to your mother to ask for a snapshot of your family. Ines, leaning over my shoulder, instructed me how to word my request, "Make sure you say that Ulrike's eyes must show. She has such beautiful eyes."

I did as Ines told me to do.

Isaac has just come up the stairs, placing his feet heavily. He's continued on up to the third floor, to our bedroom. I don't know if he's found what he was looking for, but now he has come back down and gone into his study.

Isaac is a bit taller than Gustave, a bit lankier. His eyes are a fierce blue. His beard, now mostly grey, used to be a dark blond. It's the sort of restrained, neatly trimmed beard sometimes called a Vandyke. Isaac's taste, whether in clothes, furniture or art, is austere. He admires spareness. But there is much more to him than his severity. He has an eager, clever sense of humour. Together we've laughed ourselves into states of utter silliness.

Isaac's mother was a Latvian refugee who, at the end of the war, found her way to Canada. No one would have guessed, least of all herself, that she'd marry a Jew, but that is what she did, and the immediate outcome of her outlandish behaviour was Isaac, who has spent much of his adult life examining his divergent family roots and the period of gruesome tumult that threw his parents together.

First he studied his Jewish side. The year he turned thirty, he travelled to the Polish town of Keltz, which his grandparents had fled after the Russo-Japanese War, and there he projected portraits of his grandparents onto the remaining doors and walls of what had once been a shtetl. He photographed the stones and mortar now veiled by a transparent cheek or nose, the upper corner of a shop door pressing through the left lobe of his grandmother's forehead.

In his forties, Isaac turned his attention to his mother's experiences in the DP camps of southern Germany. It was because his DP project was being shown in Berlin that we came and ate dinner at Nürnberger Strasse.

Isaac's work. It is easier for me to describe his work than to describe him, the man, my husband. He is not my husband. He has never married me.

I irritate him in so many small ways. How can he forgive me something so large as Ines' death? What allowed him to accept my obsession with your father? Or was he less aware of how I felt than I believed? No. He was as aware as he wanted to be.

I know Isaac too intimately to imagine that I understand him completely. But I can tell you about his father, Yehuda.

Isaac's paternal grandfather, Naftule, was a Jewish barrel-maker who fled Poland for Canada in 1910, having no wish to be conscripted by the Czar, not for a second time. Already he'd fought in the Russo-Japanese war. That was enough. He brought his wife and four children to the New World, where he produced five more heirs, then died of an infected thumb. A few months later his wife died also. Isaac's father, Yehuda, the youngest child, was placed in an orphanage, where he lived from the ages of nine to sixteen.

Yehuda attempted to escape his new home by unscrewing the hinges of cupboard and closet doors. He hoped his agility with a borrowed screwdriver would prompt the directors of the orphanage to expel him. The doors, falling off, made a terrific noise, but he, Yehuda, was forgiven.

Yehuda dreamed of living in a house with a garden. He excelled at school, at sixteen won a scholarship to study history and modern languages at McGill University. The year was 1941. While a student, he joined the Canadian

Officers' Training Corps; and in 1944 he headed over-
seas, a lieutenant in the Canadian Army. He fought in
Holland and by good luck survived. He met up with some
British Intelligence officers, who took an interest in the
fact that he'd studied German at university; and when the
war ended he was briefly assigned to the British sector of
occupied Berlin.

Are you surprised to learn that nearly everyone in this
letter has a connection with Berlin? Life is full of such
coincidences, don't you agree?

When, in the winter of 1945, Yehuda's time in Berlin
came to an end, he returned home to Montreal determined to study law.

He burrowed into his task; but in the cafeteria below
the law library he fell in love with a girl whose prettiness
made it hard for him to think straight. Her name was
Valda. Her job was to serve the food, the meat and potatoes, the overcooked vegetables, the soup. It did not take
her long to decide which of the students might be most
willing to help her with her English lessons. The one who
ate slowly, his eyes following her.

Yehuda graduated, was called to the bar, won Valda's
hand, worked hard. He bought a narrow rowhouse for his
bride. He worked harder, bought a wider, more ample
house. Wasn't that what Valda wanted? Apparently not.
Perhaps it was attention or passion, even intimacy that she
craved. Her unmet expectations, tenacious vines, wrapped

themselves around Yehuda. Uncomprehending Yehuda. He had no idea that Valda was also being strangled, that she did not understand her longings and expectations any better than he did.

The new house had a front yard and a backyard, both large. Yehuda released his children, Isaac and Ruth, into the backyard and waited for them to revel in their freedom. They were five and three years old. They circled each other distrustfully on the grass, snake and dog.

On Tuesdays, Valda did the laundry. "If your father . . ." Valda muttered under her breath. Slap went the iron. "If your father . . ." She twisted round the collar of Yehuda's shirt. "If your father . . ." Slap. The steam hissed and curled. When every wrinkle in Yehuda's shirt had disappeared, she turned her full attention to her children and spoke with her whole breath. "You are free," she announced, "to prefer your father."

In the evenings, Yehuda read the paper. When he'd finished, he folded the paper, put it aside, took out one of the previous week's papers, spread this on the floor, then polished his shoes.

One Sunday, on at least one Sunday, Yehuda, having mowed the lawn, trimmed the hedge, wiped his forehead with his handkerchief and admired the green expanse of his domain, went inside and knocked on Isaac's bedroom door. "Son, I'd like to have a word with you. Tell me, why don't you and your sister get along? When I was your age, I longed for a house that was my own, a house with a yard. I want you to be kind to each other."

That same evening, or on some other evening, while serving supper, Valda exclaimed, "A yard? A garden? We were seven families in one room. Displaced persons. They hung up sheets to give us privacy. Those priests, you should have seen what they got up to. Yehuda, you don't need so much salt."

One of Isaac's first acts of rebellion took place on Halloween. Valda had sewn him a cape, which he refused to wear. "I'm not angry," she shouted at him. "If anyone is, you are. Don't wear the costume I sewed for you. No one is saying you have to like it. No one is forcing you to go out and collect candies. How was I to know you hated green? If you told me anything."

Silence, Ulrike, don't you agree, is a useful skill? He fought her with silence. Mothers must sometimes be fought with silence.

She signed her children up for piano lessons, enrolled them in the Saturday Morning Club at the Royal Ontario Museum, took them skating. She slipped her one question into their food, sewed it into their clothing—in place of a label with their name—her one question: "Do you love me? Do you love me the best, above anyone else?"

Ulrike, you must not place too much faith in my accounts of Valda. My sympathies lie with Isaac and Yehuda.

Isn't there a saying in German, "When a woman marries a man, she also marries his mother"? Sometimes when I am looking for a pair of scissors, I picture Valda on her living-room sofa, her quick hands wielding her sewing scissors, her dainty feet in two elegant shoes planted firmly on the carpet. She was a woman who took great pride in her shoes. Isaac has described to me more than once what he saw when he walked into his parents' living room one afternoon, the summer he turned nineteen. His mother, seated on the sofa, cutting her old wedding dress into little pieces, tossing the scraps like so much white confetti or seed onto the carpet. He stared at her for a moment, then turned and left the room.

That was the summer Isaac was working in a chocolate factory. His clothes, even his hair, reeked of mint. When he could no longer abide the smell of mint, he left for England with a friend. He found work in a butcher's shop, then in a pub and eventually in a photographer's studio. From England he made his way to Spain and from there to North Africa. He drifted from one country to the next. There were plenty of young people doing as he was, some irrevocably lost, some in the throes of discovery.

Isaac stepped into my studio a few minutes ago. "A bit of sleep," he said. "A little bit of sleep would do you good. Why don't you take a nap?" But he's not been sleeping either. Last night, again, he went out late. When he came home, he opened my studio door and told me I should get some sleep. "It's already morning," I said, and together we went down to the kitchen. The sky was growing lighter, and as we stood there, saying nothing, a bird sang outside.

I wondered how long we were going to stand there. The number of birds singing increased, and it occurred to me that if I put my arms around Isaac we might both feel better, or alive, or something, but the thought of doing so brought a fleeting picture of Ines. She was leaning against the kitchen door frame, sucking on a section of orange and eyeing me with curiosity. She was wearing her green T-shirt, the one with the hole torn in it just over her ribs. I knew I mustn't move a muscle. Even my breathing felt like a betrayal of her. Then she was gone. I asked Isaac where he'd spent the tail end of the night. "Driving, then walking, then driving some more." I went to the sink and turned on the tap. I filled a glass with cold water, which I drank while Isaac left the kitchen. Before coming up here to continue writing to you, I glanced into the dining room. Isaac, the newspaper open, his chin resting in the palm of his left hand, was printing a word in the little vertical boxes of a crossword puzzle.

Isaac is a photographer fascinated by the context of images, the subjectivity of record-keeping. To create his installation on the displaced persons camps in München, Augsburg and Bad Worishofen, where Valda, her father and her two sisters were housed at the end of the war, he travelled to the sites.

Valda, at the age of sixteen, fleeing the Russians and the fighting that was advancing toward her family's farm, walked to the southern border of Latvia, crossed Lithuania, then Poland, on foot, and continued on into

Germany. At first she and her sisters were accompanied by both of their parents. But when they arrived at the Latvian border, their mother refused to take another step forward. She insisted on turning back, on trudging all those kilometres in the direction they'd just come from, to check that the animals they'd left behind were secure. Valda and her sisters pleaded with their mother. "You want to check on some cows? You'll be killed. We've come all this way . . ." But she would not cross the border. "I'll catch up with you," she promised.

"Come," ordered their father, and he herded his daughters forward. For another two months they walked.

Not until twenty years later did Valda's mother at last leave Latvia. She flew in an airplane to Toronto, Canada, where her daughters, now married women with children of their own, greeted her stiffly. It was they, along with their father, who'd filed repeated requests with the Soviet and Canadian governments that this woman—their mother—be permitted to join them. At last they could ask her, "What sort of woman abandons her daughters?" But they did not ask.

Instead, Valda, one afternoon while standing in her mother's scrubbed Toronto kitchen, opened her mouth and released a torrent of insults and recriminations that her mother returned in kind. For three hours they stood on the yellow linoleum, hurling their despair at each other. That is how Isaac tells it, blending what he's heard at various times from his mother and his grandmother. When they'd both exhausted themselves, Valda buttoned her coat, picked up her purse and went home to make supper for Yehuda, for Isaac and Ruth. "For your Jewish family," said Valda's mother and lowered herself onto the stool nearest the kitchen table, where the potatoes for her own supper lay waiting to be peeled.

As Isaac photographed the buildings in which Valda, his aunts and his grandfather had lived as displaced persons, he searched for any remaining clues, any evidence that the buildings had housed, at the end of the war, hundreds of people who waited, suspended, from year to year, the children and young people attending makeshift schools, everyone hoping some country would offer them permanent asylum. Except for a few gravestones in a local cemetery, he found no evidence. Several rooms of the Funk Kaserne were now used as studio space by an art school. A large fibreglass foot stood in the corridor, a bicycle leaned against the wall. He photographed both the giant foot and the bicycle.

Yes, a bicycle. I am surrounded by bicycles, Ulrike. I write the word and Ines climbs on, she rests her foot on the pedal. The car is brown, a Toyota.

The second building was in Augsburg. It was a low-rise apartment block. A white duvet, being hung out to air, spilled from a window. Isaac photographed the solidity of the building, the clean window frame and the bulky, pale bedding emerging from the dark interior of the room.

In Augsburg, Isaac also documented the arched entrance to the courtyard of an elementary school. There, a boy was filling his pocket with gravel.

Isaac scribbled down the comments of passersby who stopped to inquire, "Why are you taking these photographs of our window, of our entrance, of our exit?"

Isaac noted that on his last morning in the spa town of Bad Worishofen, the owner of the guesthouse where he was staying served him an extra hard-boiled egg with his breakfast. Isaac took this to be a gesture of farewell and photographed the egg.

In Canada, he interviewed Valda and his aunts, each one separately. Each insisted she didn't remember a thing about the camps. So he gathered the three of them together in one room, and straight away they became eager to speak, each woman determined that her own particular memories be recorded as the truth.

"Mrs. R pulled back the curtain, and there was the priest, caught between Mrs. V's thighs."

"Mrs. V? I didn't see any Mrs. V. The priest, he was masturbating, there was no one else in the room, he had a small mirror propped against the wall."

"Alone in the room? When was anyone ever alone? Don't you remember how many we were, ten on our side of the curtain?"

"Fourteen. And the noise of snoring. Some people, how they snored. That man who coughed all the time. Perhaps they'd sprayed him with too much DDT."

"And if they hadn't sprayed? We were covered in fleas."

"You had lice."

"Who didn't? I don't remember that."

Isaac titled his DP work *Everyday Life*. It included old snapshots from the time of the camps, smiling young men and women, arm in arm, whirling in a circle, in a muddy yard. The new photographs, those taken by him, revealed starkness, not a person in sight, though the buildings were in full use.

Isaac's work. His work and my work, how have they influenced each other? He is patient, thorough, encourages rigour. I am impulsive, but have become a perfectionist in my work. I expect I would have become a perfectionist in my work with or without Isaac.

Much of my work hasn't excited him. "Why should it?" he asks. "Your work is good work, often very good. It needn't always appeal to me. You're not sculpting for me."

"Of course I'm not. But when you like my work, it pleases me."

"Many of your pieces I like a lot."

Isaac's photographs very rarely include a person. I, on the other hand, once sculpted sixty small clay heads, which I arranged on the floor, in the manner of a Japanese stone garden. I sculpted seven tall, thin women, two of them pregnant, and stood them in a closet.

—

I was disturbed by the lack of people in Isaac's DP photographs when I first saw them.

"The boy collecting gravel. Was there really no one else? No one in any of those buildings you visited? You spoke with people. Did you want everywhere to be empty?"

"I didn't choose. No one was there. Only the boy . . ."

"And he's tiny."

"I wasn't using a camera well suited for capturing people. To get the entire courtyard and all its details . . ."

"So you chose."

"Yes, I chose. Of course I did."

"You chose to make him small."

"I chose to photograph the courtyard. He's the size he happens to be relative to the space he's in. Come on, Beatrice. What's this all about?"

"Either it's about you, you feeling small and lonely and not wanting to admit it, or it's about me, me wanting more attention from you."

He looked at me with a mixture of irritation and affection. For several seconds we stood, smiling at each other, at our familiar impasse, smiling with our eyes.

About a week ago, when I'd not yet started writing to you, Ulrike, I came out of my studio, where I'd been sitting, doing nothing, and I saw through the open door of Isaac's study that he was not there. I could hear the radio playing in the kitchen. I went down. He was pouring himself a whisky. I buried my nose in his neck. I wanted the smell of his skin and nothing else. It is a loamy, heated smell that pulls me out of my thoughts and roots me in the earth.

What role has Isaac played in my life? In bed, his feet warm my feet, his stomach warms the small of my back, his hands wake my breasts. Together we produced a daughter.

I have changed pens and am writing to you in blue now, instead of black. This is because a few minutes ago I heard a loud thump and a cracking, shattering sound in the hall, and I put down my black pen, which now I can't find. But what pen I'm using is of absolutely no importance.

When I stepped out of my studio, a few minutes ago, Isaac was standing on the staircase. He'd purposely swung his fist, with considerable force, into the wall. Broken plaster lay at his feet. I looked at the plaster and heard again the sound of breaking in my head and felt relieved. It was good to hear something being broken. "Are you all right?" I asked.

"My fist hurts."

"Can I get you anything? Some ice? Can I do something?"

"No, you can't."

He continued down the stairs, and I followed him. He sat on the sofa, rubbing his wrist, opening then closing his fingers. I brought him ice cubes wrapped in a dishtowel.

"I'm sorry," I said.

I did not need to ask why he'd punched the wall. Ines is dead, and I have shut myself in this room, writing to you. When we do communicate, it is wordlessly, in the dark.

"I'm sorry," I repeated. I went over and kissed his cheek while he continued to examine his hand, turning it this way and that. He did not raise his eyes to meet mine. If he had allowed our eyes to meet, perhaps it might have done us both good. But he is lonely, grieving and furious. Neither of us has the strength to do anyone much good right now. There is no point in my coming out of this room.

"I'm sorry," I said again, and I came up here and found this blue pen.

I first met Isaac when I was twenty-seven, and working as a translator for a pharmaceutical company. In my evenings I sculpted and attended classes at the Ontario College of Art. We met at a party. We stood together on a narrow balcony. As we spoke, a flock of pigeons beat their way upward through the pale evening air. Isaac told me he was engaged in freeing himself from a marriage that had become a wound. "She's gone back to Argentina," he said with relief.

Isaac's wife, before leaving, locked all her possessions into one room of their apartment, then went down into the street, where a taxi stood waiting. She asked that Isaac promise to look after her possessions. She flung her request like a silk scarf around her neck as she climbed into the taxi. She didn't seem to know that Isaac had learned to hate her, that if she'd lingered a moment longer, he might have yanked the silk tight around her throat and cut off her breath, using a fabric spun from the thread of worms.

I'm describing the moment of her departure as I have always seen it in my head. Isaac told me (not on the balcony where we met, but years later) that once, when he and his wife were arguing, in a parked car, he put his hands to her neck. It was dark out, and he tightened his grip. Someone happened to walk past, and he dropped his hands, but his fury had carried him close to killing her. That only a chance event had prevented him from becoming a murderer frightened him. Over the following years, he withdrew inside himself while continuing to live with her, hoping she would leave. Eventually she did.

The taxi pulled away, and Isaac went quickly indoors, unscrewed the small metal plate securing her padlock to the door frame of the room she'd filled with her possessions. He yanked, and the door opened. Inside the room, he found his guitar, a silver infant's cup, given to him on his first birthday, four porcelain dinner plates belonging to his sister, all buried amongst his wife's clothes.

He'd been searching for his guitar for weeks, had asked her if she'd seen it. She'd denied any knowledge of its whereabouts. How and when had she got hold of his sister's dinner plates? He turned his silver infant's cup over several times in his hand, wondering what weakness in himself had allowed him to live for so long with a liar and a thief.

During one of our long walks, more than a year after we'd met, he asked me, "Why did I go on living with a liar and a thief, year after year? What was wrong with me?"

Once Isaac and I had become lovers, I helped him dispose of her possessions. I stood knee-deep with him in her dresses and skirts, folding what she'd worn, filling each plastic bag to the brim. I pressed with my full weight until the last hiss of air escaped. I tied the neck of each bag in a knot.

She'd been gone more than six months and hadn't yet written to tell him what to do with the mounds of clothes she'd acquired over the years at garage sales and from the Salvation Army. He'd been living with one room of his apartment unusable; he'd been keeping his promise, and was tired of doing so.

We knelt in her shirts and jackets, reached into them up to our elbows. We sold her pants at the St. Lawrence flea market, her silk dresses to the chic vintage stores on Queen Street. I would have kept her clothes and worn them, had they fit me. But her shoulders were narrower than mine, her breasts more full and her legs less long.

One afternoon Isaac carried her love letters in a shoebox down three flights of stairs, out the front door of his building, and dropped them into a recycling box on the sidewalk. Some of the letters were from a former colleague of Isaac's, a photographer whose work Isaac had admired. Her lover's words, the scrawl of his desire, lay exposed in the warm sunlight, bared to the noises of the street. We walked back into Isaac's building and climbed the stairs from floor to floor until we reached Isaac's door.

"Did you read his letters?" I asked.

"A few."

"You knew she was receiving them?"

"Of course."

"Did you confront her?"

"Not over his. He'd moved away."

"There were others?"

"Plenty." Isaac opened the door of his apartment and we stepped inside. "In her eyes, I was responsible for all her behaviour. If I'd loved her, she claimed, if I'd loved her enough, she wouldn't have allowed anyone else to, she'd have dropped them all."

"Did you love her?"

"At first, yes. Passionately, or so it seemed to me. By the end I detested her."

"Did you have affairs?"

"Two or three."

"And?"

"They were my revenge. They were supposed to make me feel better, but they didn't. I disliked myself even more."

"And her? How did she react?"

"She'd get drunk, she'd call her friends in Argentina. She'd ring up an incredible phone bill, telling them how terribly I treated her. Once, I had to sell two of our chairs to pay her phone bill."

"What was she like when you first met her?"

"Sweet. Vulnerable. She was living with a guy who slapped her around. She showed me the bruise on her ribs where he'd punched her."

"And you thought you'd save her?"

"Something like that. She was a wanderer, a magpie. Her father, who was an army officer, had forced her to go to a school run by nuns. She'd had no freedom, she said. The nuns were cruel to her. Then her father died and the family lost all their money. I used to wonder if her father was really an officer. Did he die, or was he still alive, somewhere in Argentina? Possibly everything she told me about her family was a lie. It's likely, though, that she was taught by nuns. She had an incredible need to seduce every man she met."

Isaac is standing in the morning sunshine, talking with our neighbours from across the street. I can't see if Isaac is smiling, but I expect he's being cheered up. There, our neighbours have gone indoors, and Isaac is headed off down the street. He is going somewhere.

A moment ago, I was standing on a balcony talking with an Isaac I hardly knew, while pigeons beat their wings in the clear evening air. That evening, the evening of the party where I first met Isaac, whatever room I went into, Isaac appeared. It felt surprising and delicious, to be followed and found.

When I was a child, I would escape to the back steps of our house, if somehow my emotions had been bruised, and I'd say to myself, "Mom will come and find me." She came, but never quickly enough. While I waited, I'd make a tiny sculpture, using grasses or stones, paper or cloth, anything I could find in the yard or in the back porch, and then, if she still hadn't appeared, I'd take my offering to her, confident it would receive her praise.

It was a small miracle to be followed by Isaac, that evening, from room to room. The party ended and we went our separate ways. Though he'd asked for my telephone number, he did not call. Several weeks passed. I looked up his number in the phone book. I would have called him, but on the day I looked up his number our mutual friends threw another party and we met, on the same balcony as before.

We stood and laughed. At what? Perhaps someone was parking awkwardly in the street below? It was madness to feel so happy about standing on a cold, ugly metal balcony together. We stood, face to face and happy. It was then Isaac told me that he'd fallen in love with a friend of his cousin's. Apparently his source of happiness was quite different from mine. I looked over his shoulder to see which of the women in the living room was the one he loved.

"She's not here. She's gone home to visit her parents in Oslo."

"When did you meet her?"

"A few days ago."

"And you're in love with her?"

"Yes. I think so. I feel as if I am."

"Oh."

I walked away from him, through the crowded living room to the bedroom where I'd left my coat on a mound of others. By the time Isaac caught up with me, I'd pulled the zipper to my chin, tied my scarf around my neck and was tugging my hat down over my ears.

"You're going?"

"Yes."

He could see I was going.

"Where are you going?" he asked.

"I don't know. Home, I suppose."

"Can I walk with you? If you're going to the subway, could I walk with you?"

I raised my shoulders in an expression of indifference. Of acquiescence?

Isaac pulled on his jacket and we left the party without saying goodbye or thank you to anyone.

In front of the lighted subway station, with its glass doors and metal turnstiles, its escalators carrying people up and down, I pulled him against me and kissed him. What did I care if he was in love with some woman from Oslo whom he'd met a few days before? Whom he'd found attractive in his confusion, in his eagerness to forget his wife who'd just left him, who'd set him free.

It had been more than five years since I'd met a man who truly excited and intrigued me. There had been Gustave, on my parents' island, followed by the university boyfriend whom Gustave had predicted would come into existence.

With that young man, my first serious boyfriend, my first lover, I'd explored Europe, hurtling down roads in the cars of strangers. We'd rooted ourselves in gravel shoulders, under a fine rain, our thumbs pointing for hours, across sodden, beautiful fields of rapeseed or sugar beets that inevitably sprouted a distant church spire.

That boyfriend was long gone. He'd been followed by others, but by no one whose eyes saw far enough inside me, whose eyes promised to demand nothing short of the truth, whose body's proportions made me as hungry as Isaac's did, and as Gustave's had when I was seventeen.

Have you read the tale called *Tamlin*?

A young woman falls in love with a young man who climbs out of a well. He tells her he cannot stay, that he must return to the queen of the fairies, but that on a certain night the fairy queen will ride through the woods accompanied by her entire retinue, and that he will be riding at the queen's side on a white horse. "My face will be covered by my visor, but I will wear only one glove and leave my other hand naked as a sign, so that you will recognize me. If you want me to be yours, you must pull me from my horse, then hold on to me with all your strength, because the fairy queen, using dark magic, will struggle to keep me. I will become fire in your arms, next a biting snake, then a tearing wolf, but you must not let go. Can you do this?" "Yes. I can," the young woman answers, and on the correct night she pulls him from his horse.

Only when Tamlin has burned, bitten and clawed her is he restored to his true, utterly naked self. She wraps him in a cloak she has brought with her for that purpose and takes him home.

Isaac and I stood in front of the subway station.

"Is it possible to be in love with two people at once?" Isaac asked me, when we had released each other from our embrace.

"I don't know," I answered him.

He seemed to want me to say something more.

"And you are in love with her?" I asked. "This woman from Oslo."

"Yes. I'm quite sure I am. But I want to see you again."

Isaac wrote down my number, and a few days later he called me. We went out for dinner in a Japanese restaurant and used our chopsticks to measure how much sake was left in our slender china pitchers, as if we were checking the oil in a motor.

We stepped out of the restaurant's simplicity and warmth, out of its papery brightness, into a damp November evening and walked in any direction. We talked about our parents and siblings, a war that was being fought far away in the Middle East, the best film we'd recently seen. By then we were chilled and wandered in to a bookstore. We pulled book after book from the shelves, comparing our heroes—Blossfeldt, Goldsworthy, Rothko, Rodin.

Outside, on the sidewalk, he took my hand and we walked to the subway. His bus was pulling in, and I had to wait for a train. "Goodbye."

"Goodbye."

It was nearly a year before we saw each other again.

Ulrike, tell me about yourself. Do you live with someone or alone? Besides your music, what are your principal interests? On a Sunday, if the weather is fine, do you go to the Tiergarten, to Museum Island, or do you flee Berlin for the countryside, now that it is possible to do so? Do you get up early or sleep in?

Is it possible for you and me to become friends? I confess, I've started to think of you as my intimate friend. You mustn't believe I don't have friends, here in Toronto. On the contrary, I have good friends, and when they call I let the phone ring, and if Isaac is home he answers, and if he's not, the telephone continues to ring. Eventually it stops. For several seconds after it has stopped I can still feel them pulling at me, looking at me, asking me to speak, to reveal, to respond.

In one of his letters, your father once told me how he discovered injustice. He was a boy, and his mother took him with her to visit a friend of hers who lived in a large old apartment in Geneva. While his mother and her friend sat in the living room, drinking their coffee and tangling themselves, as adults do, in words, he explored the rest of the apartment.

In a bedroom he found a wardrobe and in the wardrobe a tall mirror with panels that opened out. When he stood in front of the mirror, he saw that he was surrounded by himself, that he could not escape his ugliness. His ugliness, he decided, was a form of injustice. Why had he not been born handsome? What other forms of injustice existed in the world? Which could be fought and which couldn't?

He resolved to compensate for his ugliness by dressing, from that day forward, with as much style and elegance as possible, and to fight injustice wherever he encountered it.

The men we love, Ulrike, but cannot hold in our arms, they are balloons. We've filled them with our breath. When is the right time to let go of the string?

A few weeks after Isaac, Ines and I had dinner with your parents and you and your sister in the apartment on Nürnberger Strasse, I sat down in my studio, took out a piece of paper and wrote to Gustave:

"I love you. I've loved you since I was seventeen. Of course, I don't know you very well, but that has not prevented the passion I feel for you from accompanying me on my long journey to the present state of happiness in which I live my life with Isaac and Ines."

It was best to admit how slightly I knew him, to confess that my imagination had filled in a great deal. How often had Gustave and I seen each other? Not often, but enough for me to believe that he wouldn't be impressed by imprecision, by anything shy of the truth. I wrote, "I have hoisted you like a flag."

How did I expect him to respond? I imagined he'd be flattered, perhaps amused to find his suspicions confirmed. Surely he'd guessed, that evening on Nürnberger Strasse, when he announced in front of everyone how he'd pursued me on my parents' island, when he'd looked down the table and asked me if I remembered his attentions, and I'd uttered my blushing assent while staring at my plate; surely he'd guessed from the small, damp maps my sweating hands had left on every surface in his apartment, and from the giddiness in my voice, that I was in love with him, and had never really stopped being in love with him since the age of seventeen. Did he understand that I could love two men at once? He'd spent the evening holding court, displaying his wit and gallantry, weaving between silliness and erudition, then suddenly rooting himself in warmth and a compassionate seriousness that made his whole performance feel real, not a performance at all, but the irrepressible release of his complex self. I wanted to know for whom he'd been performing; for me? And if it wasn't a performance, what role had I played in compelling him to reveal his true being? In the weeks following our visit to Nürnberger Strasse, I tried to convince myself it had all been a game, or yet another trick of my imagination. His letter to me would be brief. He'd point out, with regret, what a busy man he was. He might mention how unfortunate that our families lived so far apart, since our daughters seemed to have taken to each other, despite the difference in their ages.

I waited for a month. Then his letter came. I held its weight in my palm, felt its unexpected thickness between my fingers, then tore it open. I was alone in the house. I stood in the front hall, reading. Partway through, I went up to my study and closed the door, Isaac and Ines being due to come home shortly. I sat down.

He'd started on the back of a postcard. Two young eighteenth-century French revolutionaries were marching into the future. The painting, said the fine print, belonged to Berlin's Gemäldegalerie. One of the revolutionaries was a nobleman, slender waisted, fine featured, feminine, the other a peasant youth, a bit more solid but light on his feet.

"Here we are, marching, in the time it takes to write a letter, into what future? I can't say. You are the noble and I'm the peasant. Can I, equipped with the wisdom you so generously and misguidedly attribute to me, send you a recipe to put an end to a passion? No. Because I don't want to send you any such recipe. On the contrary . . ."

His handwriting was difficult to decipher. He'd used a fountain pen, and the letters flowed quickly. The dots on his i's couldn't keep up. They fell anywhere along the word. What was the difference between his u's and his m's? He must have been writing fast, not allowing himself to hesitate. I read each sentence over several times.

"When I met you on your parents' island, your personality seduced me, but you were young and, I sensed, quite frightened of me. That is why I hesitated to write to you, and having hesitated lost my nerve. When we next met, it was at my mother's house above Rolle, in Switzerland. You were travelling in the company of a young man, a fellow student. As for me, I was newly married.

"I remember that evening clearly. As I crossed the room, I smashed my thigh against the corner of a table, a table standing where it had always stood, just to the left of the doors to the garden. Why hadn't I seen it? I stood there, rubbing my thigh and staring out at my father's rose bushes, which were being battered by the wind.

"He'd been dead since I was a teenager, but I still considered them his rose bushes. What a wind, how portentous, I thought. Portentous of what? Of some approaching loss? Beatrice I've already lost, I told myself. Look how happy she is with her boyfriend. But she was never mine in any case.

"My wife, who is very intuitive, sensed my unease, and after you and your boyfriend had left she asked me many questions about you.

"Beatrice, my dear Beatrice, should I be telling you all this? Can I be sure you didn't intend your letter as a joke? Men don't receive such letters, not unless they are characters in a nineteenth-century novel, and even then they must be handsome.

"Yet your tone is entirely serious and straightforward. Perhaps you intended to send your letter to someone else? No. It is here under my eyes and unmistakably addressed to me. And so, my beautiful Beatrice, I must believe what you have written to me.

"I once came close to telling you what my feelings were for you. This was years ago. You were travelling alone. I'd taken a year's sabbatical and was living in Geneva. My daughters, Ulrike and Ingrid, were very young. My mother called to tell me you were staying with her for a few days before going on to Italy. Yes, I think Italy. I promised her I'd try to come by, but my weekend filled up with commitments.

"Late on the Sunday, I managed to take a detour while driving to Lausanne. My youngest daughter, Ingrid, who was in a foul mood, I left in the car with my wife, Gerda, who was herself not feeling well. I brought Ulrike in to meet you. For all of five minutes we stood in my mother's hall. Beatrice, do you remember? You'd bought my daughters candied almonds. You were perhaps twenty-nine or thirty. I'd ceased to be young at an early age. You'd taken the step of starting to study sculpture. You were on the brink of embracing your true vocation, and you were radiant.

"The following day I telephoned and invited you to have lunch with me in Lausanne. Together we visited the Musée de l'Art Brut.

"In those rooms filled with the art of mad people, it seemed possible to say anything. In the presence of those large heads made of seashells, in the presence of a panel of wood carved with a prison soup spoon, taken from some poor inmate's cell, what couldn't be said?

"What I'd felt for you on your parents' island formed into words I was about to pronounce. Then we stepped out of the museum, into the midday sun, and it was obvious to me that my confession would sound crazy to you. I spoke to you of other things. Seated across from you on the bright terrace of the restaurant (Le Poisson d'Or?), eating my soup, I wondered who was the more mad, the prisoner who'd used his spoon to gouge carvings into the wall of his cell or me, incapable of imposing my feelings upon you.

"My dear Beatrice, at present, as you rightly admit, you don't know me well, and that is a good thing for me. Your disillusionment will come soon enough."

Page after page. I counted them. Ten pages of words addressed to me by your busy father. They represented time he'd not spent reading or lecturing, conducting research, playing the piano or kissing your mother, time he could have spent in conversation with you or with your sister. Was the beauty of his words increased by the fact that I'd stolen them from you?

I held the lovely weight of his letter in my right hand, passed it to my left, then back again, unfolded it and read again from the start. I studied the spirited faces of the two young revolutionaries, their eager feet, their raised arms holding up flag and sword, their muscular calves. "Here we are . . . marching; into what future?"

Gustave ended his letter: "I am free and available to come and speak with you about this matter, if you wish. If you prefer to leave things where they now stand, then I thank you for having had the courage and generosity to write to me. I am carrying inside me and savouring a secret felicity."

I looked about for somewhere to put the letter. There was a cardboard box on my shelf. It held a few snapshots I'd taken recently of the stone faces and figures sculpted above the entrance to the Royal Ontario Museum. I took these out, put in Gustave's letter and closed the box. I thought of Icarus, plunging downward, having flown too close to the sun, and I started to cry uncontrollably.

Why was I crying? From now on, nothing would be as it had been. All that I'd lived was about to end. I was falling backwards through all the anguish I'd ever experienced. I was tumbling into a purifying heat. The letter, his letter, lay shut inside a box. But I had read it, and inside me it was unfolding.

I wrote to Gustave and told him to come to see me as soon as possible. He replied that I'd done well to choose an honest Canadian for a husband, not a duplicitous European like himself, and that he would arrive in the last week of May.

I met him at the airport and drove him to a friend's apartment. My friend, who was out of town, had left me her keys so that Gustave would have a place to stay. A place where I could visit with him in private.

He set down his small suitcase in the dining room. At the airport I'd offered to carry his suitcase, but he'd laughed and held on to it tightly. We stepped from the dining room into the living room, which was full of sun.

The remainder of the afternoon and the entire evening were ours to do with as we pleased. Isaac had to teach; Ines was being collected from her afternoon kindergarten by a friend of mine. I'd also arranged for a babysitter to arrive at 6:30.

"May I?" Gustave asked, loosening his tie.

"Of course."

He folded his tie, slipped it into an outside pocket of his suitcase, then clapped his hands together. "Shall we go outside? Shall we take advantage of the lovely weather?"

"Yes," I said.

How else could I answer? I wanted to unbutton his shirt, unbuckle his belt, untie his shoes—to undo him. But he had suggested we go out for a walk. We stood on the landing while I locked the door, then he followed me down the steep stairs and out into the street.

As we walked, our shoulders bumped together. The chestnut and the catalpa trees held up their white candles. We sat on a bench, in the garden of a large Victorian house made into a museum. Behind our shoulders the long arm of an ancient oak reached sideways through the air. The house stood white and pristine, preserved in all its out-dated elegance.

"Why didn't you write to me sooner?" he asked.

"I did. Eight years ago. After we visited the Musée

de l'Art Brut, and ate at the Poisson d'Or. But I never sent it."

"You should have."

"Should I?" I laughed. "What difference would it have made?"

"I was younger then."

"You were married and had children."

"I'm married now and have children, and I'm old."

"Don't be an idiot. You're not old. Forty-nine isn't old."

"Eight years ago you had no child. That would have made a difference."

I didn't answer. I was thinking that I hadn't sent him my earlier letter because, back then, my sculptures and my daughter, my accomplishments, hadn't yet come into existence. They hadn't yet made me his equal. It was the existence of my daughter and my sculptures that had freed me, this time, to act.

"When I read your letter," Gustave continued, "I thought there must be some mistake. But my name was there, in ink. If you'd sat down beside me and told me the same things, I wouldn't have believed you. I thought for a long time before writing back."

"I know."

"But I didn't think for too long, or I would have been immobilized."

I smiled my approval of his having taken action, of the spring air, of the open space surrounding us.

—

We stood up and wandered into the tiny orchard to the west of the garden. As we strolled under the blossoming apple trees, I started yawning. I hadn't slept well. I'd stayed awake, worrying that Gustave would not sleep on the plane and would arrive too exhausted to go out to dinner, that some obstacle would prevent us from pursuing what we'd planned. Dinner was planned. All the rest, what mattered most, what I wanted most, could not be planned, not without being diminished, or so I believed.

"You're tired?"

"I'm sorry. I haven't been sleeping well." I glanced down at my watch. "We should start back. A friend of mine has brought Ines home from school. I must be there before the babysitter arrives. And then we'll go out for dinner?"

"Yes, we'll go out for dinner."

Ines showed Gustave around our house, then the babysitter arrived and Gustave and I were free to leave. We returned to the apartment where he was to stay the night. Our dinner reservation was for nine o'clock. Seven had seemed too early and there'd been no table available at eight. I couldn't stop yawning. Gustave told me to lie down on the sofa and rest. I did as he told me to do.

He went out on the balcony to smoke a cigarette, then he came in and walked down the long hall to the bedroom at the back of the apartment. When he returned to the living room, he smelled of cologne. I'd already sat up and was waiting for him. He carried a present in his hands, a book on the painter Paula Modersohn-Becker. He sat down beside me. I looked at the cover of the book, then turned and kissed him quickly on the mouth. For an instant I wondered what I'd done. Wasn't I a seventeen-year-old and he a professor from Berlin? I lowered my head. But he put his thumb under my chin and lifted my head. Then we kissed each other fully. No other kiss had existed anywhere in the world before ours. We tapped our foreheads together, tentative, testing the hardness of bone. We seemed to disbelieve in the power of our skulls to separate us. He brushed his cheek across mine, and his skin felt soft. My lips devoured the borders of his mouth. We discovered the hardness of our teeth, the strength and precision of our tongues.

"Shall we skip dinner?" he murmured. I pulled my head away from his in order to think.

"No," I said. "We'll go out for dinner."

He shouldn't have addressed himself to my mind. My mind grabbed at our plan to eat dinner and held on. The air surrounding us had become thin, dizzying. The air of Mount Olympus. We were gods. When I was seventeen, I'd imagined down to the last detail how he would kiss me. His thumb would lift my chin. Now his thumb had done so, proving that time was nothing but a kaleidoscope, a small tube to be stared into and turned, so that the coloured events, caught inside, might fall into new patterns.

But despite his thumb, he'd asked his question and my mind had behaved as a mind ought to. It had searched for the truth, questioned, examined the evidence, it had said, "Gustave lives in another country. You've no right to take Ines away from Isaac. You could abandon Isaac. Or could you? That is not, of course, what Gustave is asking you to do. Or is it? Not one square inch of solid land will remain. Many will drown."

While I pulled on my shoes, Gustave's hand found my thigh and remained there. Then we both stood up and walked to the door. He pushed in the little button that controlled the hall lights and said, "There, now we're in the dark."

The words *Yes. Let's skip dinner* formed in my belly, but my tongue refused to articulate them. I wanted to show him I was capable of not wavering. He was a man who, I imagined, admired decisiveness. I'd given my answer, I'd abide by it. I told myself that we still had lots of time, that after dinner we would come back.

"You needn't turn the lights off," I said. "We'll be coming back."

He raised his eyebrows. "Not for several hours. There's no point leaving them on while we're out."

After dinner, we climbed the narrow stairs, unlocked the door and entered the apartment. A telephone sat on the dining-room table. At the sight of it I dialled my own number and heard Isaac's voice. I asked if he had paid the babysitter, if all had gone well, if Ines was in bed and asleep. "And you," he asked, "will you be home soon?"

There was something heavy waiting at the edge of his voice. Tiredness? Anger?

"Soon," I promised. "I'll be home shortly."

I set down the receiver and walked over to Gustave. He was seated on the sofa. I sat down beside him and we took hold of each other. But he whispered, "Beatrice, if you're going, you must go now or I'll take you to my bed." I freed myself and went home.

My daughter has died and I'm telling you about Gustave. And Ines? Is that what you're wondering? Very well. Her eyes were as dark and extraordinary as yours. What else? She had thick eyebrows, a pretty mouth, Isaac's strong nose. There. That's the best I can do.

Fine dark hairs grew from her spine, right at its base and between her shoulder blades. Delicate, dark hairs she detested. When she was a toddler, I saw them and suspected that one day she'd hate them. The birthmark on her left thigh grew longer as her thigh grew longer. I don't know why this surprised me.

She was small for her age, then shot up at seventeen, just as I'd done, late for a girl. When she was a child, like most children, her body gave off tremendous heat. Her hair was blondish brown and straight. I insisted her hair be cut. I refused to allow it to grow down to her shoulders. I could remember sitting in agony while my own mother combed then braided my unruly hair. I didn't want to have to wrestle every morning to impose order on my daughter's hair.

She was three years old. There was her breakfast to prepare, her clothes to pull on, her shoes to tie and her teeth to clean—enough; I wanted something to be simple.

Ines took clothes pegs and clipped dishtowels to either side of her head. The dishtowels hung defiantly down to below her shoulders. One white with blue checks, the other yellow with green flowers. She'd won. She'd obtained long hair. She agreed to unfasten and remove the dishtowels only when we left the house, and to go to bed at night.

None of this sounds as if I was cruel, does it, Ulrike? We rarely choose to be conscious of our cruelties.

The summer of her fifteenth birthday, Ines dyed her hair black. I told her I'd been bracing myself for a nose ring, a tongue piercing, cigarettes and pot, or worse. "You're crazy, Mom." "Am I?" "Ask Dad."

She bought herself a snake. It curled around her arm. Euripides. I got to like him. His small flat head. The smooth dryness of his skin, his fluidity. "Euripides," I'd hear her croon, curled on the sofa. "My lovely Euripides."

I'd knock at her bedroom door. "Can I come in?" "No. You can't." Half an hour later I'd knock again. "Can I come in?" "Sure." There were books piled on the floor: *Bulfinch's Mythology, An Introduction to Ancient Greek, The Oxford Latin Dictionary, The Basics of Greek Grammar, Sophocles Revisited, Sappho: Selected Poems, The Iliad.* I balanced her clean laundry on her chair. "Thanks, Mom." She spoke without looking up from her book. "This is really cool. Words keep changing shape, depending which case they're in. You start with 'Oitos,' doom or fate, go to 'of doom,' 'for doom.' There's even 'O Doom.' The change in meaning gets right inside the word. Cases are amazing. And particles are even better! They're these tiny, barely visible words. There are tons of them. They have no meaning on their own, but drop one into a sentence and it colours everything. It says, 'I'm raising my eyebrows as I write this, I want you to be surprised as you read my words.' Or a different one warns you, 'Proceed with caution, this sentence is doubtful; I'm not really sure what I'm saying is true.' Of course, some grammarians don't get it. They're totally anal and can't cope with the excitement, so they put particles down: 'Particles provide at most a minor clue to how the writer feels.' Particle bashers! What do they know? Particles are awesome. Holy shit! What a fantastic language." She grinned, she fixed me with her beautiful, probing eyes, which seemed to ask, And you, how do you measure up, are you as flexible as the word *oitos,* powerful as a grammatical particle? "Cool, eh?" she concluded.

"Yes." I slipped out of her room to prevent myself from telling her she was wonderful, more extraordinary than the whole complex structure of Greek grammar.

One night she came in very late. From where?

"What's it to you?" She spoke with such disdain that I picked up a dining-room chair and brought it down hard on the floor. One leg came unglued. "Fuck!" I pulled out the loose leg and stood there, holding the wooden limb in my hand. "Don't do this to me. You don't have any idea what it's like. Just call. That's all."

—

When she was seven, she asked me, "Mom, please, do you have to swear so much?" And at eight she asked, "Mom, please, don't make strange noises. It's very annoying."

"What sort of noises?"

"Like 'Oooo' and 'Grrrrnch' and 'Worgleworgle.'"

"Oh. Those."

"If you don't stop, I'll have to kick you," she threatened, with a mischievous smile.

"I wouldn't kick me, if I were you. Worgleworgle-blitsyfart."

Then we chased each other around and around the dining-room table.

She was a bit younger than eight when she announced, "My life is sneaking up on me. I look behind me and I can't see it, and I can't see it ahead of me either, but it's coming." Or is that exactly what she said? She frequently accused me of inaccuracy. "You say anything, Mom. 'The other day.' 'The other day.' But it wasn't. It was last Tuesday, exactly three days ago. I lost my tooth last Tuesday, not 'the other day.'"

What does any of this add up to? A grab bag, a mound of scraps, a selection of party favours. That's all I'm offering you. All I'm capable of providing. I can't describe her voice. You'll never meet her. There, I'm being imprecise. You did meet her once. But when you shut your eyes, can you hear her voice?

What do you remember of her? Will you tell me? Please tell me.

Her laugh. When Ines laughed, fairies and ogres tripped into the room, small lights skipped around a dark pond. Every year she learned new spells. Since birth she'd understood the uses of enchantment.

Her birth belonged to a fairy tale. All births do. Not to the watered-down versions but to the dark tales, the true ones, brimming over with beauty and ugliness, the grotesque pitted against the wondrous.

A creature was struggling to free itself from my flesh, to escape the prison my womb had become. Was it Him? Her? I'd been feeding it, harbouring it for months. How many heads would it have? How many legs? The midwife would cut the umbilical cord, yet I'd remain tied to it for life.

Already, I was familiar with its movements. I'd wait for them. On the stairs I'd hold suddenly still, and inside its sack the small beast held still also, waiting, listening. Which of us would move first? Already we were drawn to each other by an intense curiosity; already we were pulling back, challenging the other to make the first move. So be it.

I lounged in my bath, waited to catch in my open hand the sudden kick of a cramped foot, the bulge of my inhabitant's turning hip. I balanced the bar of soap on my navel and waited for someone inside me to knock it into the water. And what if the creature were perfect, except for its missing eye, its twisted spine, what then? I would have to face myself. And who would I turn out to be?

—

Ines was kind to me. She gave me one quick warning, then started her journey, which she completed in less than seven hours. I reached down and my fingers touched her head. It was soft and damp and slightly hairy, and it was forcing its way out between my thighs. Not moving into me, as a man would be in his desire, but out. I moved my fingers out of the way of her determined, vulnerable skull. It was not, of course, my fingers holding her in, but the stretched and burning rim of my vagina and the taut skin of my perineum. We both pushed. She shot straight out and the midwife caught her.

A while later—a "while" without shape or form, as if a dam had burst and the room were flooded with time, minutes moving in any direction—she grunted like a piglet and, following the scent of my milk, nuzzled her way to my breast. As she latched on to my nipple with her toothless gums, I gasped, imprisoned in a pain more intense than any I'd felt during the preceding hours.

When she'd drunk her fill, she lay on her back, her small body wrapped tight as a parcel, in soft blue cloth, arms abandoned at her sides, limp down to her wrists, but fingers curled tightly in on themselves, clutching some secret brought from elsewhere, dark lips slightly parted, smooth cheeks flushed, eyelids lowered, lungs filling, milky breath escaping—the envy of Venus.

Within a few days we'd regimented time back into minutes and hours, coins of time we added and subtracted but no longer had the authority to spend as we pleased. Ines raised a skeptical eyebrow above one eye full of knowledge and observed us.

"Where have you arrived from?" I asked her.

"How long has she been awake?" asked Isaac.

Certain questions would now dominate my existence: "How long has she slept?" "When will she wake up?" "Will she sleep again?" "For how long?" "Must I squeeze my independence into this one hour?" "How am I to breathe, corseted within an hour?"

"Love set you going like a fat, gold watch," said Sylvia Plath to her newborn child. This attempt of mine to describe Ines has failed. What I describe, I destroy. It is changed into something else. She cannot be described.

Are you a mother? Forgive me, Ulrike, for not having asked sooner. I've been stupidly assuming you're not. But perhaps you have a fairy-tale birth of your own to tell—a miscarriage, an abortion, the delivering of twins, a Caesarean section, a stillbirth caused by strangulation? Has every word in my long description of Ines' safe arrival, of the miraculous ease of her birth, caused you pain? I am sorry if that's so.

How little I know of you. I hope you've never conceived without wanting to, or failed to conceive when you did want to.

Must I imagine you, suddenly, with a child? It's too great a jolt. I'll wait and see if you write to tell me that I must include a child in my picture of you. For now, I'm leaving you childless.

Certainly if you'd had a child that Gustave knew of, he would have written to me. But you were only twenty-two when he died, and now you are twenty-eight. Quite a lot must have happened to you during these last six years.

This afternoon I opened the bathroom door and found Isaac, seated on the closed toilet, crying. He wrapped his arms around my hips, pressed his face into my belly. Beneath my palm, his familiar skull. The rounded bone, thinly covered. "In Balzac's time," I said, "phrenologists believed they could read a person's personality from the lumps and bumps of their skull." What else could I say? "Yes, Isaac. Our daughter is dead." He pressed his face deeper into my belly.

Tell me about your mother, Ulrike. Has she retired? She was close to Gustave's age, I believe, and were he still living, he would now be sixty-two. I expect your mother continues to run back and forth between the zoo and the university, that she lectures and publishes articles: *Five Perspectives on Methods of Reintegrating Zoo-Born Gorillas into the Wild. Recent Changes in Zoological Practice: From Berlin to San Diego.* A few years ago I searched for her on the Internet and came up with those two titles.

What fictions did Ines create from my letters, as she rode down l'avenue du Parc? I have the letters here in front of me, but they refuse to tell me anything about her perceptions of them.

I am building a bomb. I can feel its energy all through this house. It is good to feel energy of some sort in here. Soon everything will fly up in the air, torn apart, disperse itself. There will be no beginning to go back to.

What I remember of your mother is her white silk shirt, her decisive statements, the quick movements of her hands, a surprising vulnerability in her bright eyes, and the pleat in her fine white wool trousers. Then, suddenly, I see her as a child in an attic, pissing.

You must know the story. I'm sure you do. She told it to me that evening we all ate dinner together, on Nürnberger Strasse, and so much happened, though I'm not sure we knew what had happened because nothing had happened, but a great deal had been felt, and we all hugged and kissed and said how we hoped to see each other again soon.

"Before we get even older and more ravaged," your mother said, adding quickly, "meaning those of us who live in this unliveable, claustrophobic city. You Canadians aren't as ravaged as we are. In Berlin, there's no middle ground; one has too little work or too much. No middle ground exists. Is that becoming true in Toronto also?"

I noticed an old photograph that hung in a frame. It was near the doorway into the dining room. It showed a farmhouse. The roof sloped steeply, and two men were waving, leaning from the windows of what must have been an attic room.

"My great-uncles," your mother explained. "They both died in the First World War. When we were children, we played up there, in those two rooms right under the roof. One day we found an army helmet, the Kaiser Wilhelm sort with a spike on top. Tipped upside down, it made a perfect chamber pot. We stuck the spike between the floorboards and then took turns crouching. Afterwards, we emptied our urine out one of those windows where my great-uncles are waving."

How often did she really piss in that helmet, Ulrike? Once, twice, three times? I'm glad she did, at least once. What else of her do I have to hold on to? The white of her silk shirt? The impeccable pleat in her pant leg?

To understand someone, I must lower myself inside them, feeling along the damp walls for something to grip. Is the same true for you?

That evening, I mentioned to your mother that Ines ate very little.

"Are you worried?" she asked me.

"A bit," I confessed.

"The best is to let her be. Ulrike was the same. She ate like a bird until she turned twelve. Then her friends started growing breasts and she felt rather envious. She asked me when it would happen to her. I answered that if she ate a bit more, possibly her turn would come sooner. I didn't mention it again. She started to eat, and these last two years she's grown considerably. If you oppose Ines, you won't win. A child with her will and imagination? You won't stand a chance, not in a battle about eating. It could become serious—not about which foods, but about eating at all."

Did your mother blush, or was there a subtle change in the rhythm of her breathing that caught my attention? I don't remember. But I sensed a sudden disquiet in her. She rearranged her knife on her plate.

"There." She leaned toward me, her tone not anxious, as I'd expected it to be, but amused, "Ulrike's been listening. She's heard everything. Do you see? They hear everything." I turned. You were standing in the doorway behind us.

You walked across the room, took a pair of scissors and a roll of string from a drawer. What were you and Ines making together? Do you remember? Will you tell me?

Your mother, Ulrike. Your mother. I used to go into our living room in Toronto, mine and Ines and Isaac's, and sit down for a moment on the sofa. I'd do this before going to collect Ines at school, having just washed the clay or plaster from my hands. I'd sit for several minutes, savouring the emptiness of the house, the two silent floors above me and the basement below.

Sounds came from the street, a nanny calling to a child, the beeping of a truck backing up, then nothing until the furnace clicked and warm air blew from the vent in the corner. Your mother would walk in without warning, in my imagination, and ask me, "Have you slept with Gustave?" I'd have to answer.

Sometimes her voice accused me, but most often it was unbearably innocent. Yet if she suspected nothing, why was she asking? She'd stand there, in her white silk shirt and finely tailored white wool pants.

It wasn't when I'd just received a letter from Gustave that she'd visit me, but in the weeks after I'd answered, when I didn't know what he'd make of my response or whose hands my words might fall into; that was when she'd arrive, when I was wondering if I would ever hold him naked and feel him enter me.

Isaac never asked me, "Have you slept with Gustave?"

Suppose he'd asked me, "Are you lovers?" Would that have been a different question? What are lovers who cannot act?

This morning, very early, Isaac and I woke. We pressed ourselves together. We made love; we entered each other through our mouths, our chests, the backs of our knees, the paths of our ears. We were in all these places at once. Ulrike, we were everywhere. We were inside each other's belly and at the back of each other's throat. I flopped onto my back. My skin smelled of Isaac, and my mouth was the shape his tongue had given it, and I felt happy for one moment, for one appalling moment, full of the obscenity of survival, of the joy of discovery. Then I curled myself in a tight ball and struck at the mattress repeatedly with my fist. Isaac asked me to stop. I whacked at the mattress harder. Again he asked me. And so I stopped, and lay with my fist clamped between my legs.

When Ines was five and you, Ulrike, were fifteen, I wrote my longest and most frequent letters to your father. Why didn't Isaac ask me to stop? At least once I started to cry in the middle of dinner. Surely he knew why? Or did some instinct of self-preservation prevent him from knowing?

"Are you all right?" he asked, his eyes probing.

"Yes. I'll be fine."

"Is it your work?"

"Something like that."

"You look exhausted. Why don't you go up and lie down?"

"What about Ines? I promised I'd read to her after dinner."

We often discussed Ines in front of her, as if she weren't there. Anyone who's not fully independent, who lives under someone else's authority will find themselves being discussed in this way at times, will get used to being turned into a ghost. Most parents turn their children into ghosts fairly regularly.

"Dad can read to me," said Ines.

"Go rest," Isaac advised me. "You'll be more rational when you've had some sleep."

Ulrike, Isaac has just announced he is leaving. Not for good, he assures me. He doesn't know where he's going.

Possibly to New York. He's taking our car. He will call, or write.

There, he's driven off. I wanted to walk downstairs with him, and out, and across the street. I could have carried his suitcase. But what would have been the point? I stayed here and watched through the window.

I'm going to go outside now and see what the air is like, how cold it is. A woman has just marched briskly past the spot where our car was parked until a few minutes ago. The woman was wearing a thick scarf and hat. I won't go out. I'll go down and pour myself a whisky. Isaac and I are both alive, and incapable of comprehending why.

The one time Gustave came to Toronto, we walked arm in arm beneath blossoming chestnut and catalpa trees. We dined in a restaurant, and the following afternoon he left.

I drove home from the airport, where I'd dropped Gustave off. I drove alone, in a state of ecstatic devastation, tears trickling down my face and neck. They were real tears. Everything was terribly real—the cars in the next lane, the drivers behind their steering wheels and the passengers, the concrete divider, the white letters on the green signs indicating different possible directions to be taken, the salt I licked from my cheek, all these belonged to the same acute afternoon.

Outside my window, right now, the dark branches of the maple trees are reaching out and out through the air, with their usual daring. The tires of the parked cars have stopped but have not forgotten they were made for motion. They are waiting. As for the air, it does not appear to be moving. Isaac said he would come back. The branches outside my window have been acquiring weight and solidity as I stare at them. They reach so far out that they ought to break off but don't.

Gustave ended his visit with me by flying from here to Boston. He'd been invited to give a talk at Harvard. From Boston he wrote to me:

"Have you ever been here? Do you know this city well? How can I help but imagine, my beautiful Beatrice, what it would be like if you were here with me? Last night I walked to a restaurant, and perhaps it was because of my black raincoat or because of the way my white shirt collar and the top of my dark necktie protruded, but a drunk shouted at me as I leaned into the wind, "Hey, Father, can you spare some change?"

"Until he spoke, I hadn't paid the slightest attention to the church I was passing in front of. It had rained, it was cold, there were puddles I didn't want to step in. I was fighting the wind and looking down.

"As I ate my dinner, alone, I said to myself, That drunk was right—at heart I'm a priest.

"Why else didn't I lead you down the hall after I turned out the lights? Who but a priest would have got up off that sofa, without even trying to convince you to change your mind and skip dinner? In that last hour before you took me to the airport, I hadn't stripped the bed because I

thought there was perhaps a hope. I was also convinced
you'd made up your mind. How agile you were in the way
you avoided uniting with me. The union of two bodies
reveals the truth. Your life with Isaac and Ines is a happy
one, a life you've worked hard to achieve. No doubt if I
were younger I might insist."

He was forty-nine. "I've been old since I was seven," he
wrote. But he was lying. He'd not been old since he was
seven. I don't think he knew he was lying. He'd been serious since the age of seven, or six or four, but not old.
What of his idealism and impulsiveness? They were real.
He insisted they were the products of my imagination.

He went on in his letter to declare that all of his best
qualities were my inventions, and that the man I believed
him to be did not exist outside my fantasies. "I'm not at
all who you think I am. Besides, you've worked hard to
arrive where you are. If what you and Isaac have built
together were not so palpably successful, so happy . . ."
He ended his letter by advising me: "You must cultivate
your garden."

I answered: "I'll do as I please with my garden."

How many letters did we exchange? For every three or
four that I sent, I received one. I told him that I woke
every morning to hear him ask, "Shall we skip dinner?"
and that now my answer was, "Yes." I said that in the last
hour before I drove him to the airport I'd believed it was
he who'd made up his mind not to make love to me. How

comic, how tragic; how ridiculously we'd failed to communicate our desire. Yet why must it be too late? Couldn't
we meet again?

When his letters arrived, they went on for pages, as
generous in content as length. He praised my work, my
talent, my discipline and courage. "The future," he
insisted, "rests in the hands of the artists. Everyone else
has sold out. You must continue. Your work is what matters most."

I was pleased to be told that my work mattered. He
meant what he said, and it pleased me. But he also meant,
and wanted me to believe, that my work was more important than any love affair I was dreaming of, than any "dan-
gerous illusions" I might have about him. "I'm so far from
being the man you think I am." It was up to me to work.
In work I would find satisfaction; through my work I
would give of my vision, my humour, my understanding
to the world. My understanding? I saw no reason to
choose between my work and an affair with him.

And yes, he did tell me that I was beautiful. He was no
fool. He knew he must feed my vanity if he wanted to keep
receiving my letters. And possibly, he did find me beautiful; quite possibly, he was in love with me.

As much as I coveted his erudition and his mental dex-
terity, he coveted the elusive whatever that enabled me to
sculpt—by staring at each other we could picture ourselves
complete. It was an old story. It was old even before it began.

—

Isaac is speeding along some highway. He's not wearing a helmet, because people in cars, unless they are racing-car drivers, don't wear helmets.

Ulrike, will you read what I'm writing, or will I end up having spoken to no one? Does it matter, so long as I believe you are listening?

Ines once explained to me that when the Greeks figured out how to write, they stopped telling epic poems and turned inwards; their poetry became lyric. It was as if, literate, they'd grown more aware of their isolation, of themselves as individuals. Literate, they were forced to stare down at a page, whereas when telling their epics they'd looked into each other's eyes.

She'd wander into the kitchen, reading as she walked, literate, forced to stare down at the page. Suddenly she'd stand still, read a passage aloud, exclaim, "Pretty amazing, eh? What do you think?" Then she'd look up. Our eyes would meet. All true meetings are of incalculable duration.

At last, or perhaps it was only a moment later, she'd turn her attention to the refrigerator door, which she'd pull open. "We're all out of milk."

Ines, what do I think? I do not think. I want. I want you to walk into this room, a book or a sock in your hand. I want you to walk into this room with nothing in your hand.

Stretched out on the sofa, in her overheated apartment, Ulrike adjusted the cushions under her head.

You sound profoundly lonely. You're confusing me with Ines. If she were she still alive, I'd want to meet her. If I were to tell you that today, the day I received your letter, I saw an eighteen-year-old girl reading a book in Greek while waiting for her boyfriend in a café, that this girl had straight, blondish-brown hair and dark, inquisitive eyes, would you think I had seen a ghost?

Your husband, Isaac, may return only to collect his belongings, but I hope he comes back to stay, and that he does so soon. You want to know if you and I can be friends. I'm not sure on which page you asked, but you did, and I was tempted to say yes; and then you started describing, again, your sexual feelings for my father. I couldn't tell you to stop; and you didn't stop, and I continued reading.

Ulrike rolled onto her side. The oppressive warmth of the room weighed down on her. She thought of getting up and opening a window but didn't. Anxiety and the heat made her listless. She lay in her cocoon of stuffy air and felt she hadn't slept properly in days. After several minutes of lying still and with her eyes shut, she found herself in her parents' bathroom. Next to the tub stood Beatrice Mann, dressed in black jeans and a peacock blue turtleneck. Gustave came in. He set his briefcase on the floor, then slipped his hands up under Beatrice's turtleneck. He was standing behind her. He unfastened her bra, then his hands moved forward along her ribs and took hold of her breasts. Next he was peeling the blue turtleneck up and up, until Beatrice's head disappeared inside it. Ulrike looked down at her watch to see how old she was. The long hand pointed to twelve and the short hand to three. That means I'm fifteen, she thought. She glanced up again, in time to see Gustave press his face between Beatrice's naked breasts. Ulrike had seen men do this in movies. She watched as Gustave's mouth searched for Beatrice's nipple, and found it. She did nothing to stop what was happening. She wanted to see what this man, who looked so like her father, would do next, to witness a culmination. But the scene stopped abruptly. Ulrike put an end to it by slapping down the letter she held in her hand. It hit the hard edge of the bathroom sink with a resounding whack. And all the same, it was too late. What she'd just witnessed had made her Beatrice Mann's accomplice in a crime against her mother.

The telephone was ringing in the kitchen. Ulrike opened her eyes, recognized where she was and ran to stop the ringing.

"Ulrike?"

"Hello, Max."

Darjeeling, appearing out of nowhere, pressed his lean flank against her shin. Ulrike bent down and, with her free hand, scratched him between his ears.

"Are you okay? You sound upset," said Max.

"I am. I've been reading a letter."

"Who from?"

"A woman my father knew."

"And?"

"I'll tell you about it when you get here."

"I'm stuck in traffic. That's why I'm calling. Every road in this fucking city is being torn up. Oh, fuck."

"What is it?"

"Sorry. I just missed a chance to get out of this lane, and now there's a bus in front of me. I'd better ring off."

"Goodbye."

"Oh, God."

"What is it?"

"A woman on the sidewalk is taking off her clothes. She'll freeze. She's got her shirt off and now she's working on her pants. People are staring at her, then walking on."

"How old is she?"

"Hard to say. Thirty, forty? Either she's mentally ill or seriously stoned, or both. She can't get her pants off because of her boots. I've got to go, the bus is moving."

"Bye."

Ulrike pressed disconnect, set down the telephone, took a glass from the cupboard above the counter, filled it with cold water and drank. She wondered if by now the police had come and taken away the woman Max had seen from his car win-dow, and if the woman had succeeded in yanking off her boots so she could free herself of her pants before they arrived, and how coldly the snow had pressed against the soles of her feet. Max was caught behind a bus, but being Max, he'd slipped deftly into another lane and got away.

A mournful Turkish love song came swimming through her kitchen wall, then drowned in a wave of static as someone changed channels in the apartment next door. She heard a thump. A large object had fallen. It had fallen on the floor of the apartment above. But there'd been no sound of breaking, and no one was screaming or swearing. Ulrike cut herself a slice of bread, a piece of cheese, and returned to the living room. Her mind was full of breasts, the back of her father's head and a blue turtleneck, from which someone else's head was about to be freed. She could feel her fifteen-year-old self watching, holding her breath. But what she'd just dreamed had never really occurred. She'd never come upon Beatrice and Gustave beside the bathtub, nor anywhere else. She was quite sure she hadn't. She picked up the page where she'd left off, read a sentence but felt thirsty. Reading as she walked, she headed back to the kitchen.

ULRIKE, IF YOU WERE standing in this room, and if I were speaking not writing, would I be telling you this story, or a different one?

Before Gustave left Toronto, I asked him if it wouldn't be better that I send my letters to his university address. "We are allowed to write to each other," he answered me, his voice hard. It was the first time I'd heard anger in his voice: "To write to each other—that, at any rate, we've every right to do. No one but me will open letters addressed to me. Anyone who opens and reads a letter not addressed to them deserves to discover whatever's inside."

I did as he told me to do. I sent my letters to "Gustave Huguenot, Nürnberger Strasse 24." Was it sometimes you, Ulrike, who handed my letters to him when he came home from work?

I don't think he had anticipated how often I'd write, how bulky my letters would become. He soon added a postscript to one of his own letters: "I suggest that, from now on, you write to me at my office." I threw back my head and laughed. Men!

Hadn't I warned him that he would not enjoy being surrounded by suspecting eyes, no matter how strongly he believed in his right to receive whatever letters he pleased? What use was his understanding of the intricacies of Habermas, of Adorno and Horkheimer, if he couldn't foresee the obvious? From then on, I sent a portion of my letters to his office, and a portion to Nürnberger Strasse.

The wall that divided your city in two—were you in the crowd of people I watched on television, the night of November 9, 1989? Some were straddling the wall, others stood at its base; some were singing, others swung hammers, chipping off chunks to take home. I looked for you, for a fifteen-year-old girl with brilliant dark eyes and Gustave's fine nose. I looked for your mother and your sister. While the news commentator chatted joyously in my ear, I searched for Gustave but couldn't find him. I didn't really expect to find him in such a swarm of people.

"I failed to foresee what was coming," he wrote to me. "What has been the use of anything my colleagues and I have written if we couldn't smell what was fermenting right under our noses? Yet the wall has fallen. Beatrice, this is great cause for celebration. Every citizen of East Germany is free, or so I'm tempted to say in my excitement. But that would be a lie. Though most East Germans are, in a sense, far freer than they were last week, in our sad world we have no true freedom to offer, only the wildly unequal freedoms enjoyed by the citizens of Western capitalist countries. We are not nearly so free as many would like us to believe. Yet at this moment, I can't help but feel joy, and indulge in a naive hope that a better future is perhaps approaching. The wall has fallen. The wall has fallen, and I failed to foresee it."

Isaac has been gone for two days but hasn't called yet. Perhaps he will tomorrow. When he's ready, he'll call. I cannot allow myself to believe otherwise. Has he arrived safely in New York?

Very soon a pale but unstoppable light will seep into the sky, and birds—sparrows mostly, an occasional jay and a crow—will wake and make their pronouncements in the face of everything. And I will feel grateful to them for expressing themselves so clearly, for suggesting that self-expression is still worthwhile and defeat to be resisted.

Do I sound like Gustave? The heroic birds will assert their individuality while also defending the rights of their fellow birds in the face of oppression? Over the years, despite my resistance, his political thinking has affected me. But I do not sound like Gustave. The birds I hear singing, now that morning has arrived, are singing urgently about something he refused to hear.

Gustave's visit to me, in Toronto, took place in May 1989. By the following December, I felt I'd stepped off a train at the wrong station. If only I could sustain sufficient hope, I told myself, the correct train would soon come and carry me to my true destination. If my letters could move Gustave deeply, then he would come for me.

All through December and into January, my restlessness grew, my hungering and ill ease intensified. Of what importance are these dates? In December, my father-in-law, Yehuda, took to visiting us repeatedly. Was it Isaac's preoccupation with his father that distracted him from my preoccupation with Gustave? Fathers, and more fathers, Ulrike.

I could go to my shelf, open a box and find out the exact dates on which Gustave wrote to me that winter. I've taken his letters and mine from the plastic folder in which Ines was carrying them, I've transcribed sections of them for you and have returned them to their box. I don't want to open the box right now. Inside it, his letters and mine are arranged chronologically. They form a clear sequence. Ines did this organizing for me or, rather, for herself.

I have taken the plastic folder she was carrying and placed it where I can see it, on a shelf next to some books, a bowl of sponges, several large stones, a ruler and a vase. I can see it from where I am sitting.

As for the box, it is ample, made of metal, yellow in colour and decorated with a caricature of a black man, of a Moor, wearing a red and blue turban and ballooning striped pants. *Sarotti since 1852* is printed beneath the picture.

The box once contained delicious German chocolates, and was sent to me by your mother as a gift, the first Christmas after we met.

Yehuda came by train to visit us. It was a long, potentially hazardous winter drive from Montreal, so he preferred to come by train. He was barely sixty-five in 1989, but was suddenly complaining that his memory was giving him trouble. Ruth, Isaac's sister, who lived on her own in Pointe Claire, a pleasant suburb of Montreal, and met with Yehuda regularly, had expressed her concern over his growing frailty. He'd cut back his law practice to a minimum. Generally he'd arrive in Toronto on a Friday evening and travel back home on Monday or Tuesday. He never stayed longer than four days, for fear of making a nuisance of himself. He brought us presents. For Ines, who was five, a sword and shield, a large plastic cow with a slit in its back so she could drop in her pennies, a stuffed wombat that sang "Waltzing Mathilda" when you squeezed its foot, a *First Encyclopaedia of Animals,* a set of magnets, a variety of spinning tops. Perfume for me, and for Isaac, gin.

Yehuda wore cheerful sweaters, yellow or robin's egg blue and sober brown shoes. He balanced Ines on his knees and asked her, "How's my favourite grandchild?"

She didn't say, "I'm your only one," or climb off his knees. She indulged him in his imprecisions to a greater degree than she did most adults. She seemed to trust him, to sense that his love for her was true and boundless, that her existence brought him joy. It could have been otherwise.

Ines stood stiffly at attention, a small soldier, in her Granny Valda's embrace. Isaac's mother came once a year from California, where she lived with her second husband, and responded to Ines' shyness with a display of emotions as stunning as a peacock's tail. In her voice and gestures, indifference, eager attention and bruised withdrawal switched places at alarming speed. Yet a pattern existed, or so Ines seemed to hope. "Yes," she seemed to be saying to herself, "a pattern must exist within my grandmother's behaviour, and I will find out what it is." Sunk into the deepest living-room chair, Ines, from the safety of her cave, studied her Granny Valda—this small woman who wore beautiful shoes and threw her warbling voice high in the air.

Yehuda's visits were easier. If Ines was busy, up in her room or off at a friend's house, Yehuda would sit down on the sofa, open a book and read contentedly until one of us made time for him. I was oddly happy in the moments I spent looking after Yehuda, seeing to his moderate needs, that winter.

That winter, if I stood idle for more than a few minutes, Gustave's question, "Shall we skip dinner?" and my answer, "No," flooded my mind. Keeping Yehuda company soothed me.

I would come into the living room to offer him a drink, or to suggest that he join me in the kitchen, and find him sleeping, a book in his lap. Suddenly, he'd open his eyes and smile apologetically. "I must have dozed off. I haven't been sleeping much at night."

"Is something troubling you?" I'd ask, sitting down beside him.

"No, no. I've seen my doctor and he assures me all's in good working order. So long as I stay off salt and avoid fats, I'll be around a while longer."

"Of course you will."

"You two don't use too much salt, do you?"

"No," I assured him.

"I didn't think so. You're both looking well."

He often spoke to us of the virtues of a vegetable called mâche, which he'd eaten in Paris at the end of the war. Could it be had in Toronto? He'd failed to find any in Montreal. Was it still available in Paris? Did we know?

When I asked about the book he'd been reading on the sofa, he confessed it was not very interesting.

"Not nearly so interesting as *Moby Dick* would be, or so I suspect. But unfortunately, I haven't read *Moby Dick*."

"Neither have I."

We found ourselves listing the books we most regretted not having read, and from there we moved on to naming composers whose music we knew nothing about but wished we did.

That winter was exceptionally mild; instead of snow we had rain. At the end of an evening, Yehuda would pull on his old beige raincoat, walk gingerly down the front steps, turn with his arm raised, wave slowly, then step into the taxi waiting to carry him off.

No, not "off," but back to his hotel. Though I knew I would soon see him again, all of his departures felt final. They echoed an earlier absence. It was at the moment of his leaving that I felt most keenly he'd never been present.

"Is it because our spare room's so small that he won't stay with us?" I asked, though Isaac had explained his father's behaviour often enough.

"No, it's not that. He can't stand feeling indebted to anyone. His hotel room he pays for, and there he knows he's not underfoot. Why do you think he won't let me give him a ride to his hotel? He doesn't want to inconvenience me."

Repeating to each other what we both knew about Yehuda was a ritual Isaac and I engaged in, the way a dog turns in circles before lying down to sleep.

"Does he strike you as a lot older than he was a year ago?"

"Yes. He's slower, thinner, more tired, more forgetful. More like a man in his late seventies than his mid-sixties."

"Are you worried? Have you spoken with him?"

"Which are you asking me? Yes, I'm worried. And, yes, I've tried to speak with him. I've been trying to speak with him, without success, for most of my life."

—

The postman has arrived, Ulrike. He's shoved something through our slot, something that has landed on the floor.

No, nothing of interest, bills and requests for charity.

I asked you, Ulrike, at one point in this letter, to judge me, but of course you can't. Some stories are told too late, others are stumbled upon. Some are told so the person telling them can figure out why they are doing so. Yehuda had a story he avoided telling for a long time, a story he resisted.

"Son, you know that right after the war ended I was sent briefly to Berlin?"

"Yes."

"The war was over, but Europe was a mess," Yehuda explained, and then he stopped speaking.

"Dad?" Isaac asked after several seconds of holding the telephone to his ear and listening to emptiness.

"Yes, I'm still here."

"You were saying something about Berlin."

"You're not in a rush? I'm not keeping you?"

"I'm not in a rush. Tell me about Berlin."

"We were posted in the British sector of the city. My role was not a very big one. I was a small cog in the largely ineffectual de-Nazification process. I was instructed to interview Berliners, to try to determine, by means of a questionnaire, to what degree they'd been involved in the Nazi Party."

"Surely most of them had been members."

"Of course. And most claimed they'd been 'forced' to join. We gave them the questionnaire to fill out, and we tried to corner them into confessing the truth. We had little training. It was all pretty hit or miss. One day, I was listening to a gaunt, exhausted man describe how his local Nazi leader had persecuted him for refusing to join the party, when I remembered that under the Third Reich all German citizens had been issued identity cards with their pictures on them. Suddenly I wanted to know what this emaciated man had looked like when he was well fed. I asked him to show me his card, and without thinking, he obediently handed it to me. I held his true face in my hand, his double chin and his hard little eyes that stared arrogantly up at me. The swastika pin, given to party members, was proudly displayed on his lapel."

"And what did you do with him?"

"I attached his identity card to his questionnaire and passed him on to my superior officer. Then I sat down again. I sat behind my desk in that gutted building surrounded by rubble and questioned the next destitute person in line. They were mostly women. The men, by and large, were off in prisoner-of-war camps. Outside the building where we were billeted, women waited with buckets in the evening, hoping to receive slops, whatever scraps of our supper we hadn't finished."

"Dad, I'm sorry. I'm going to have to cut our conversation short," Isaac reluctantly interrupted his father.

"Could I call you back later this afternoon? I have to leave in five minutes. I have a dentist's appointment."

"I'm sorry for keeping you, son. I'll call another time."

"Why don't you come to see us? Ines would love it. And I want to hear more about Berlin."

"I think I will come down to visit you, if that wouldn't be too much of an inconvenience?"

"Dad, what sort of inconvenience did you have in mind? I just invited you."

"Yes, you did. That's true. If I were to take the train that leaves here next Friday morning I'd arrive in Toronto at 4:15. Would that fit with your plans?"

On the day following his arrival, Yehuda took Isaac out for lunch. Their conversation started over from the beginning—how Yehuda had been a small cog. The impossible task of de-Nazification. Then Yehuda started adding new details.

"Those buckets the women held out to us, son, they were the same they'd been filling all day with rubble. So many of the streets were blocked with rubble. The city was silent. No blaring horns, no squealing brakes and rattling streetcars. Many people bound their feet in rags, but some made themselves odd-shaped wooden soles. I could hear them clumping along the sidewalk, where there was still any sidewalk.

"There was an area I hated having to walk through and tried to avoid because the smell was particularly bad. Bodies were putrefying in the heat. There was no one to bury them. Every day nearly a hundred children were gathered from the various railway stations and placed in institutions. But even in the orphanages there wasn't enough food. Stalin was already doing his best to limit our access to the city. Our supplies could only trickle in, and most of the food-growing areas were in the East.

"I sat behind my desk and questioned starving people. From their answers, you'd have thought not a single Berliner had ever supported Hitler and that they'd all been against him from the start."

"What did you do?"

"Not much. I couldn't do much. There were the exceptions who gave themselves away, like that man. I think I told you about him on the phone?"

"Yes, you did. The one with the photo ID."

"A few Berliners had the courage to speak honestly, and we punished them for their honesty. What else could we do? We were right to punish those we could. I hated to think of how many I must have been letting slip through my fingers, the worst of them, no doubt. Were any of them innocent? The place was destroyed. Most of the people wandering about or foraging in the rubble looked like zombies. I did damn little. I took some food to the elephant in the zoo. He was one of the few animals who'd survived. He was nothing but bone and sagging skin, a giant skeleton ambling about.

"One afternoon a man and woman came in together. He was short and thin, with a nasty twist to his mouth and ugly ears, ears that struck me, for some reason, as being forcefully ugly. He held one shoulder higher than the other, and his eyes burned with anger. Most of the eyes I stared into across that desk were dull, barely alive. This man was a living caricature of a wily evildoer. Not a stiff, orderly Nazi. An older form of devil. The young woman who was with him, she even looked young, whereas most young women in Berlin looked old, and she was a bit less starved than most."

Yehuda stopped talking.

"And then?" asked Isaac.

"Then?"

"I thought you were going to say something more."

"Nothing urgent. Nothing that can't wait. The war was a long time ago, and we've been sitting here quite awhile. They might want this table for someone else."

"Who for? There's no one waiting."

Yehuda signalled to the waiter to bring the bill. "I'll drop you off, son, and then I think I'll just stop by the hotel for a little rest. I confess I've fallen into the habit of taking an afternoon nap."

"It's probably good for you."

As Isaac was getting out of the taxi in front of our house, Yehuda turned to him, "I hope our conversation hasn't been a disappointment to you."

"No, Dad, it hasn't. Why?"

"I'm sorry, son. I appear to be forgetting more and more. Perhaps tomorrow I'll be thinking clearly."

It wasn't until Yehuda's next visit, several weeks later, that Isaac heard more about Berlin. Yehuda's memory seemed in good working order. Cigarettes, he told Isaac, were the principal unit of currency on the black market. He reeled off the price, in cigarettes, for a kilo of bread, a sexual favour, a Leica camera. He recited the wording of a suicide note he'd read. It was pinned to the ragged dress of a woman he found hanging from the remains of a lamppost, itself half uprooted from the broken side-walk. "Frau Kom, Frau Kom, Frau Kom," then the number sixteen. He assumed she'd been raped by Russian soldiers, quite possibly sixteen times. On sepa-rate occasions? Or by a group of sixteen, lining up for their turn? In the first weeks of the city's occupation, the Red Army had had complete run of the place, and given the unspeakable treatment the Russians had received in German hands . . . It was only a guess. Who knows what that number sixteen meant? Yehuda told Isaac again how he took food to the emaciated elephant wandering about the zoo.

"And the man with one raised shoulder, and ugly ears, and burning eyes?" Isaac asked. "And the young woman who had visibly eaten better than many?"

"Did I mention them?"

"You did last time."

Yehuda pulled his handkerchief from his pocket, unfolded its square white expanse, buried his nose in it and blew.

"Perhaps you just need to talk, Dad. Maybe you don't have any one specific event you want to tell me about," suggested Isaac, though he believed the contrary. "Just lots of small events, not that they're small, maybe that's all you want to tell me about?"

"You're probably right, son." Yehuda got up. "I think I'll go catch some shut-eye before dinner." In the hall, he pulled on his rubber galoshes, buttoned his raincoat and combed his thin hair so that it lay flat on either side of his part. He stepped out onto our cluttered front porch with its peeling paint, descended the stairs, turned and waved in his unassuming way, then stepped into his taxi.

"Your poor father," I said to Isaac later that afternoon.

"Yes. My poor father. This is how it's always been between us. He gets this close, then steps back, or I step back," Isaac replied and got up from his desk. "With Ruth he's not much different, as far as I know."

"But you are talking, the two of you are at least talking; and not about some vegetable that used to be popular in Paris."

"That's true. I'm going to the corner store. I'll be back soon. Are we out of anything besides tea and onions?"

"I don't think so."

"I'll take another look before I go."

I sat down at Isaac's desk. I listened to his feet carrying him down the stairs. On a scrap of paper he'd been scribbling a fierce cross-hatching of black lines.

How often we'd dissected Yehuda, identified his characteristics: generous, passive, controlling, not altogether unhappy, distant and, we assumed, somewhat lonely.

At last Yehuda was placing in Isaac's hands these horrific scenes he had been carrying about inside himself for decades. But at the end of each conversation, Yehuda stood up, emptied his face of every trace of his own words and behaved as if nothing he'd just said had any bearing on the present, as if the act of having spoken altered nothing. Why did he refuse to leave anything to build on? Why did he insist on destroying the bond he'd created with his son a moment earlier?

"My father, the harmless *trompe l'oeil.* It's nobody's fault. These conversations are exhausting for both of us," was Isaac's summation. "For me, at any rate, they're exhausting. I can't speak for him. He's tried to speak for me all my life, guessing from inside his fantasies of who I might be. I feel sorry for him, and I can't stand this feeling of not knowing what's going on. Who were that pair in Berlin?"

In bed, Isaac told me wordlessly all he felt for his father, good and bad. What do you think, Ulrike, is sex a photographer's darkroom, where we develop the same negatives over and over, the only ones we possess? The print comes out quite differently each time.

Yehuda came to dinner the following day. "There was no mâche in Berlin," he remarked as he served himself from the salad bowl. "No mâche," he repeated, and he laughed, then he cleared his throat. His laugh was much warmer than his customary small smile. It struck me how rarely I'd heard him laugh. Perhaps he'd known all these years how ridiculous, how sad his obsession with mâche had become, and now, inexplicably, he was freed of it.

I cleared the table and Isaac put the kettle on while Yehuda drifted off, in his imagination, to Berlin. I took Ines up to her room and put her to bed. I lay beside her, waiting for her to fall asleep. On nights when she dropped off quickly, it was pure pleasure to lie with her. More than pleasure. The shape of her body, her size and warmth, her weight, the fact of her physical existence. I shaped myself to her body. Sometimes, when I'd lain with her for more than an hour and still she could not give in to sleep, I became infuriated. I suggested that maybe, at six years old, she was ready to learn to be in the dark on her own. I had phone calls to make, dishes to wash, books to read. She apologized for making such demands on me but insisted that I stay. I stayed. She knew I wanted to be elsewhere. She knew I was not elsewhere. How did her reasoning make sense of this? She'd endured my anger and won? She'd deserved my anger and been forgiven? We lay together.

On the night of Yehuda's visit, Ines fell asleep quickly. When I came downstairs, Isaac and Yehuda had moved into the living room.

"The man had a nasty mouth," Yehuda was saying.

I poured myself a cup of tea and sat down.

"I pitied him," Yehuda explained, "because he looked wretched, and had off-putting ears and uneven shoulders. But I didn't like his eyes, and I didn't trust him. He accused the young woman of having worked as a guard at Bergen-Belsen. He claimed to have met her in his aunt's living room.

"I asked him, 'When?' 'In September.' '1944?' 'Yes.' 'A bit over a year ago, then?' 'Yes.'

"His aunt, he claimed, was a seamstress who lived not far from the camp. On the day he'd met the guard, he'd come to visit his aunt because his family's cow had fallen ill. His mother had sent him to ask if his aunt could spare some milk. He'd knocked, heard his aunt tell him to come in and had opened her front door. A young woman was standing with a dress in her hands. That's what he saw when he opened the door, a young woman wearing a Nazi uniform and holding a flowered dress in her hands.

"She'd brought the dress for his aunt to alter. His aunt's nervousness surprised him. His welcoming, talka-tive aunt stared through him. The young woman was complaining that the roads between the camp and the seamstress's house were swamps of mud. 'Yes, there has been so much rain,' said his aunt, smiling and smiling. She suggested that the young woman put on the dress, explaining, 'I will be able to fit it for you much better.' But the young woman insisted she had tried it on already, that it fit perfectly, except in the sleeves and the length of the skirt. The sleeves were two inches too short and the skirt must also come down an inch or two.

"As soon as they were alone, his aunt said to him, 'That woman is a guard at the camp,' then his aunt gave him the milk that he'd come for, and he left.

"Today, the man claimed, he was standing in Unter den Linden, tying together two pieces of rope he'd found, when he looked up and saw her, the guard who'd brought the dress to his aunt for alteration.

"He'd planned to use the rope to hold up his pants, as the night before someone had threatened him with a knife and stolen his belt, but instead he stuffed the rope in his pocket, held up his pants with one hand and ran after the woman, who was walking down the middle of the road. She was carrying a tea kettle in one hand and a small suitcase in the other. When he caught up with her, he grabbed her by the arm and told her that he knew perfectly well who she was and that he was not going to let her slip away.

"He'd been true to his word, he boasted, staring at me across my desk; he'd not let her slip away, here she was. 'Do you see that mole on her left cheek?' he asked, leaning forward. 'She is the woman who was in my aunt's living room. I'm sure of it. Her face. She made an impression on me. I'd never seen my aunt so unnerved. Well? What are you going to do with her?'

"I wrote down all that the man had said. Then I asked the young woman if any of his story were true. She shook her head. I asked her to speak up. 'No,' she said. I could barely hear her, she spoke so quietly. Her suitcase and kettle sat on the floor.

"I pushed a pen toward her and a questionnaire—the *Fragebogen* Berliners were meant to fill out. The Americans made zealous use of the *Fragebogen,* insisting that everyone, no matter their age or condition, fill one out. We, in the British sector, were less convinced of their effectiveness. Still, we wanted to get at the truth and they were a tool, a blunt tool.

"She'd spent the entire war in Berlin, she wrote down. She'd worked as an assistant in a flower shop until the shop was bombed. Her father and brother had been killed at the front in the last days of the war; her mother had hanged herself; her sister was perhaps alive and in Munich.

"I asked to see her identity card. It had been stolen when three Russian soldiers had dragged her into a basement and raped her during the first week of the Soviet occupation. It had been in the pocket of the dress she was wearing, and they'd left her naked.

"Yes, she had been a member of the Nazi Party. The owner of the flower shop where she was employed had threatened to fire her if she refused to join. But she'd never set foot in Bergen-Belsen; she had no idea where such a place was.

"Who was I to believe? Likely they were both lying. She'd perhaps admitted to being a party member in order to convince me of her honesty.

"The drawer of my desk contained what we called Persil certificates. Persil was our nickname for the Allied Form. A Persil certificate stated that its holder was 'clean.' Persil was a brand of soap. Should I give her one? Her 'companion' was accusing her, and had a specific story that he stuck to without slipping up. No matter how I tried, I couldn't succeed in luring him into contradicting himself. Yet my instincts insisted she was innocent. What instincts? What made me want to see her as innocent?

"I ought to have passed them both on to my commanding officer for further questioning. But the more I looked at the young man, the more I detested him—his burning eyes and nasty mouth, his grotesque ears. He clearly wanted the young woman punished, and so I decided to thwart him, to give him no satisfaction. I filled out a Persil certificate and slid it across the table.

"'This document,' I said to her, 'it states that you are not a Nazi and never have been; it entitles you to work even in such restricted professions as teaching. Please take your belongings and go.' She stared at the paper, then tucked it inside her shirt, thanked me and hurried out the door.

"The young man was furious. I could see it took all his will for him not to yell at me. I was wearing a uniform and, no doubt, he was used to showing respect to uniformed figures. 'You let her go,' he said in a low, hate-filled voice. 'How could you? Don't you understand what she did? She should be punished. You don't believe me, but someone else will.' He demanded to speak to my commanding officer.

"Why was he, a German, so determined to see her punished? How, I asked myself, could I, a Jew, have certified her as 'clean,' just minutes ago, with no proof one way or the other, with only some voice inside me insisting I believe her miserable tale? I felt numb and exhausted. For more than a month I'd been living with all my thoughts dominated by the relentless necessity of acting conclusively on inconclusive evidence. I filled out another Persil certificate and slid it across the table.

"'Take this,' I ordered. 'It will be useful to you. Don't ever come here again. If you ever come back to this building, I'll make your life difficult.' He snatched up his certificate of cleanliness and left."

Yehuda had taken his handkerchief from his pocket several times while he spoke, now he pulled it out again, blew his nose and apologized.

"I hated that little man. There was something about him that got under my skin. She was pretty and quiet, and he wanted to destroy her. I couldn't stand him. But what if he was right? When they opened the camps, they found thousands of dresses. Why would he have made up such a story? Why mention his aunt, the seamstress? Perhaps his story was true, but she was the wrong woman? I wanted to believe in the Berlin flower shop and its Nazi owner who pressured her to join the party; I preferred to believe in the Russian soldiers who'd raped the young woman sitting in front of me than to believe she'd ever set foot in Bergen-Belsen. Did I hand a Persil certificate to a concentration camp guard? To a pretty one? All I had to do was to pass them both along to my superior officer, but I couldn't. Suddenly I wanted to decide for myself, to act according to my feelings, to follow my own intuitions and nothing else. All of my intuition told me to distrust this angry, ugly man, and to pity this quiet young woman."

We sat in silence, Yehuda, Isaac and I. Then Yehuda stood up.

"Well, son. Your father's done some pretty stupid things in his life."

"What you did wasn't stupid."

Yehuda's small smile appeared. "That's kind of you to say so. It's time for me to turn in. I don't need as much sleep as I used to, but you two have had a long day, and you have a busy one ahead of you tomorrow."

"What you did wasn't stupid. I think you are far too hard on yourself, Dad. Tomorrow we'll discuss it further?"

"I'll just get my coat from the hall."

In bed a few hours later, Isaac lay on his back, his head supported by his pillow, hands clasped on his stomach. "Do you think it made Yehuda feel any better?" he asked.

"To have told us?"

"To have told us as much as he did."

"Was there more?"

"There's always more."

"Perhaps for a few moments he felt better. I hope so."

Isaac wrapped himself around me, just as I had wrapped myself, earlier that evening, around Ines, and we slept.

We received a phone call from Yehuda, mid-January, during the course of which he mentioned in passing that he was going into the hospital the following day, for a colonoscopy.

"Better safe than sorry, as the saying goes. For men my age it's quite a standard procedure. I've read several articles, and it seems to be recommended. Not a pleasant way to spend an afternoon, but there won't be much to it."

"In which hospital will they do it, Dad?"

"Montreal General. I go in at noon and will be home the same day."

"Will Ruth collect you?"

"I've told her not to readjust her schedule, but she says she's going to anyway, whether I like it or not. And she's filled my freezer with enough cooked meals to last me until the spring."

The procedure went smoothly. Yehuda called to assure us that he was home and not in any discomfort. Ruth, he said, would be having dinner with him the next day.

The following evening, Ruth telephoned. Yehuda had died a few hours earlier. His heart had failed him. She'd let herself in, expecting to find him setting the table or fussing at the stove. Yehuda was lying curled on the kitchen floor.

For a week we sat shiva, while Yehuda's candle slowly burned.

At the start of this letter, Ulrike, I hoped you would issue me a certificate—not a Persil certificate—but one declaring my guilt, a punishing certificate. What I want from you now is your friendship.

Max took the stairs two at a time on his long legs, quickly unlocked Ulrike's door and walked in. "Hello?" he called out.

She came from her bedroom, some papers in her hand. He took her in his arms, pulled her tight against him, held her just as he'd imagined doing while he was climbing the stairs, each stair falling behind easily, conquered by the muscles in his calves, and her door coming closer in the heat of the stairwell, which seemed oppressive, enclosing, after the expansive cold of the street. The moment he'd reached her landing, he'd tugged open the zipper of his jacket while fishing with his free hand in his pocket for the key.

He kissed her on the mouth. The stiffness of his new shoes, which were not yet worn in and had rubbed at the back of his left heel, the steam he'd watched coiling up and out of the hot water that covered his stomach as he'd lain in his morning bath, as best he could, knees bent, and the arguments Fritz, the violinist from his trio, had presented him with, over the phone, three hours ago, in defence of Haydn versus Mozart, all these rushed to his lips not as words but as desire. Ulrike received his tongue hungrily. Grateful, light-headed, he continued to kiss her, then, separating his mouth from hers, he took a small step backwards so he might look at her.

"I'm glad your rehearsal was cancelled," she said, smiling.

He was studying her face. "You look tired."

"Do I?"

"Yes. Are you sure you want to go out?"

"I want to go out. I wonder what happened to that woman you saw stripping on the sidewalk?"

"I don't know. The traffic started moving. I had to go forward. The roads are a mess. It's getting worse. I hope someone managed to help her. She must have been freezing." Max pulled off his sweater. "Christ, it's hot in here."

"There's something wrong with the system. It was worse earlier this evening. Or I've just got used to it. If they haven't figured it out by the time I get back from Düsseldorf, I'll have to get after them again."

He looked down at her hand. She was still clutching the pages covered in someone's inky chicken scratch that she'd been holding when he'd strode in and taken her in his arms. "Is that the letter?"

"Part of it." She dropped the pages on the sofa.

I don't want to explain, she thought. I need to go outside. Suddenly, intensely, she wanted movement and noise, every sort of purpose pulling people, pushing them up one street and down the next. If there was to be no order. . . . Her coat and hat were hanging from their hook beside the door. She pulled them on.

"Let's go."

"Who's the letter from?" Max asked, watching her.

She'd finished buttoning her coat and was tugging her mittens out of her pockets. She said, "It's from a Canadian woman who had an affair with my father. Now her daughter's died in a cycling accident, and to complicate everything, when her daughter was hit by the car she had my father's and this woman's letters in her knapsack."

"And she's telling all this to you?"

"Yes, she is."

Ulrike turned the knob, the bolt slid over with a satisfying clank and the door swung in and open. "Her daughter was eighteen."

"Christ," said Max, and he followed Ulrike out onto the landing, yanking the door shut with a bang behind him. "Traffic must be just as bad in Canada as here."

She stared at him. "You can't help it, can you? Everything's a joke." She was smiling.

"Sorry. It all just sounds so weird. The letter, I mean. And the rest is just plain awful."

"You're right. It is awful, and weird."

As they galloped down the stairs, she took hold of Max's hand. They stepped out onto the sidewalk.

"How about the Jassy?" she asked him.

"Sounds good to me."

They walked quickly, saying nothing, and reached the corner, then turned onto Prenzlauer Allee and along the quieter Christburger Strasse, and now, thought Max, I can ask her more, more about the letter, more about everything, now that she's out in the fresh, cold air she was craving. He'd discovered, in the year and a half he'd known Ulrike, that his faults included untidiness, prying into what didn't concern him and wanting to teach Ulrike to relax. She didn't want to relax. She wanted to play at "Make Max a Better Person." He didn't mind, not for now. It was a game. In his bathtub, he'd fantasized, just today, that under her influence he might indeed become a better person, more thorough, or more ambitious. But he had no real intention of changing. He rather liked himself the way he was. And as for Ulrike, she was not so serious as she thought herself to be. Of this Max felt certain, more certain tonight than ever before. Tonight she was behaving with an impetuous eagerness he believed belonged to the "true" Ulrike, the Ulrike only a privileged few were allowed to glimpse. Her mittened hand, as they walked, tightened its grip on his, let go, squeezed again, sending him muffled signals, a woolly SOS.

"Are you going to write back to this woman?" he asked.

"I don't know."

"What sort of person is she?"

Ulrike tried to explain what sort of person Beatrice was but failed. They turned up Husemannstrasse. The street lights seemed to her unusually bright. But perhaps this was due to the clear, dry coldness of the air. She would have been happy to explain but couldn't. For once she wanted to explain. But the more she tried, the more confusing it all sounded.

"You'll have to read it yourself," she announced and let go of his hand.

"Do you want me to?"

"I don't know. You want me to have all the answers. I've always been expected to know everything."

They'd arrived at Café Jassy. Max pulled the door open and they stepped inside. The room smelled of coffee, beer, soup and everyone's warm breath. Two speakers, connected to a CD player behind the bar, were releasing frenetic Romanian wedding music, dizzying as a wasp in a jar, some virtuoso gypsy weaving on clarinet. The room was full of talk that climbed over, pushed its way through the music. Every table was taken. They stood as near to the bar as possible, then Max, sliding sideways, managed to lean in and order. A moment later he turned to her, grinning, in either hand a foaming glass of beer, and he was off, manoeuvring his way toward a table that was suddenly free. She followed him in a state of tiredness that felt like happiness. She sat down. Took a long swallow of beer and dropped out of the café, so to speak, through a hole in Beatrice's letter, straight into a hospital room where Gustave lay, a white sheet pulled up to his chin.

Max drank quickly, then slowly. He set down his glass. He leaned back in his chair and watched Ulrike's face, her throat and chest. Sadness, inescapable as any weather system, was moving in. He saw it climbing up through her, invading her shoulders and neck, overtaking her mouth, filling her eyes. He hadn't expected this. He'd prepared himself for wit, a jousting match.

"Are you all right?"

"I'm all right."

He smiled at her tenderly. "Is that why you're crying?"

Tears were running unimpeded down her cheeks. Max fished in his pocket, hoping for a tissue, but could feel only something small and hard, which he took out and discovered was a packet of chewing gum. The tears had reached her chin. She wiped them away with her sleeve and more came.

"I'm thinking about my father."

"Ah."

"I was in his hospital room, the morning he died. I was the only one there. I'd arrived before my mother and sister. I walked over and said hello. He didn't open his eyes. I hadn't expected him to. I looked at his mouth. It was open and very dark inside. His lips had bled. There were cracks in the skin of his lips. Because he couldn't swallow and was only receiving water through a tube in his arm, his tongue and lips kept drying, splitting open, bleeding and drying. Whenever we came to visit, we wet his lips and tongue, and the inner walls of his mouth, with a swab. The nurses supplied us with the swabs. But at night we weren't there, and the nurses didn't have time to keep his mouth moist. They had plenty of other patients. My mother had been staying with him most nights, but because she was exhausted Ingrid and I had insisted she give herself a night at home, to rest. We thought he had several days to go, and we planned, from now on, to all stay with him, if possible, twenty-four hours a day.

"I looked on the table beside his bed for a swab, but there wasn't one. I could hear the scraping, pushing effort of his breathing. It filled the room. Lying on his back, he was working hard—as hard as a snowplough clearing a street after a storm—but there was nothing mechanical about his efforts; he seemed more human than ever. I was about to pull up a chair when the sounds he was making changed. His breathing became frantic, but in slow motion, as if he was reaching for something just beyond his grasp. He was like a child who's taken off the grate and shoved his whole arm into the vent into which he's seen something small, belonging to him, roll down and disappear. And then he stopped trying, and the sounds he'd been producing stopped.

"His silence frightened me. I was quite sure he was dead, and I didn't want to be the only one who knew. Surely, I thought, I should have done something to save him, to save myself. I pressed the buzzer beside his bed, and a nurse came. I stepped aside so she could search for his pulse, or do whatever she needed to do in order to tell me that he was dead. When she turned to look at me, her face was full of pity, and I wished she weren't there. I turned my back on her, walked to the door of the room and saw, beyond the nursing station, my mother and sister, stepping out of the elevator, hurrying along, bringing books and food, everything we'd need to occupy ourselves while keeping my father company, while waiting for him to die."

All through Ulrike's speech, Max couldn't take his eyes off her. He examined the shape of her nose, the bone of her cheek and the malleable flesh of her earlobe. He put out his hand and touched the only part of her he dared, her hand. It was resting on the table. He covered it with his own.

ULRIKE, THE POSTMAN IS COMING up our steps. No. I was mistaken. It was only a young man delivering junk mail.

Perhaps it is time I described this room to you. Its bay window offers a view of brick houses packed tight as passengers on a streetcar that has come to a standstill, and above these houses maple trees explore a margin of sky. An old woman is standing to the left of my desk. Her fingers are silver teaspoons, her spine a fishing rod. I brought her home from my workshop several years ago. She's one of the few figures I have room for in here. Two dented pewter ashtrays form her breasts. Her arms are dangling Slinky toys. That she has no head doesn't mean I have anything against heads. An entire corner of my studio downtown is occupied by a series of clay heads, some as large as ostrich eggs, some small as a hen's. Each balances on the tip of a tall, slender metal stem. There used to be a forest of these heads-on-stems that you could walk through.

They weren't gruesome. They weren't impaled. Think of a forest of tall flowers.

"Mom, if you want the idea of a stem rather than a spike, a few of the wires have got to be thinner, more pliable, so that they bend a bit under the weight of the head."

Ines had strong, clear opinions about my work. The second time she walked through my garden of heads, she stated emphatically, "I think the most beautiful head is this one." She was right.

"Look at these blossoms," said Gustave. "Unbelievable. In Berlin we've had rain, endless cold rain, no sun, no spring. And those birds hopping on the lawn. I've started to notice birds, Beatrice. I'm becoming sensitive, at last. A few years ago I would never have noticed those birds." His fingers tightened around mine. Two linked hands. The rope connecting climbers. Which of us was the more sure-footed? We had to collect his suitcase from a room with a bed. For an hour we would be alone. We'd never seen each other naked. His departure was bounding toward us, teeth bared. "Do you realize how incredible it is that this encounter has happened?" he asked. "Do you know what the odds are against such a meeting between two people?" Our blue amazement spread above the catalpas; did anyone, passing us and staring up, mistake it for the sky?

Opera, Ulrike. My encounter with your father was opera at a whisper. This letter is intended for your eyes only. If you read it aloud to someone else, or give it to them so that they may read it, the letter will be changed.

Haven't you found this? After you've shown someone a letter, the letter is no longer the letter it used to be. If it was a fast-running stream, it becomes a pond; if it was a pond it becomes a fast-running stream. The light on the water alters. It is never again the same letter that you read to yourself, that no one but you knew the depths and temperatures of.

I don't remember on what day in January Yehuda died, only that it was January, and that all through the month of January, that year, Gustave's profile, his nose and forehead, were printed overtop every one of my thoughts. In the middle of the day, while I waited to pay for my groceries, Gustave would reach out, in my imagination, and place his hands on my shoulders. He'd look at me, then unbutton my coat and slip his hands inside.

I was sculpting small wire figures—they all had Gustave's proportions, his buttocks and shoulders, his legs. Six of the wire men sat on park benches, their arms stretching east and west along the back of the bench. I'd seen your father sit in a Toronto park, wearing black pants, an immaculate white shirt and brilliant blue suspenders, beneath a blue sky, the shouts of children in the playground, the rumbling of streetcars, leaves rustling in the wind, all of these noises circling him, your silent and sober father, pinned to the bench, arms stretched between east and west.

—

One afternoon in February, I watched Ines and Isaac come walking along the sidewalk in front of our house. I observed them through the living-room window. They came up the concrete path leading to our front steps and started to climb. Then they unlocked the front door and entered the house, which was clearly theirs, the house in whose living room, by some accident, I was standing, holding a pear in my hand.

All that winter I could not concentrate on my work and squandered my time in my workshop. More than once, while preparing supper, I turned from the sink, saw Ines staring at me and realized I hadn't heard a word of what she'd just said to me. One afternoon, when I should have been collecting her, I lost track of time and they called me from her school to ask where I was. I wrote to Gustave and asked if I might come to see him, to complete what we'd begun. I told myself that if I made love to him, I could free myself of him, that in one act of union I could love him sufficiently to last me a lifetime.

The postman has just slid something through the slot downstairs. It has landed on the floor of the front hall with a lovely sound of finality.

Yes. I have it in my hands. A letter from Isaac. Would you like to know what he says? I want to transcribe it for you; and I don't want to.

Dear Beatrice,

I'm writing to you from the Sleepwell Motel, about an hour's drive south of Buffalo. I was too tired to go any farther. This room's the sort no one would want to stay in more than a night or two. It reeks of failure. What colour did the carpet used to be? Your guess is as good as mine. The dresser is particularly ugly, with ornate metal handles that are small and difficult to grip. The drawers stick and squeal. The top of the dresser has been gouged by sharp objects and burned in several places.

I came in the door, dropped my suitcase on the floor, myself on the bed, then got up again and walked over to the dresser. I can't imagine many people would bother to unpack in a room like this.

I've taken a shot of the dresser. It's the first photograph I've taken since Ines' death.

What are we to do, Beatrice? The obvious answer is, continue. But how? Supposing I could find the driver who knocked her off her bicycle and kill him? Or I could try cursing God?

The only thing I can do, in fact, is miss her, go to bed missing her and wake up missing her. I'm sorry I've left you on your own, for now.

You've always wanted something from me that I couldn't give you. You know all this. Sometimes you stop asking, but then you start up again.

Now Ines is dead. When she died, you wanted me to tell you it wasn't your fault. It wasn't; and I told you so. What more could I say? But you wanted more. I tried to work. I sorted through old files, marked student's assignments, tore up a grant proposal I'd been preparing. Halfway through destroying it, I stopped feeling so childishly furious, and kept on tearing the papers for some colder reason. I felt horribly cold and had to put on another sweater. I wanted to talk to you, and I didn't want to. I wanted Ines. Then you started your letter to Ulrike. I could sometimes hear you in there, crying. When I'd open the door, you'd turn, with your pen in your hand, and look at me. But whatever I said was not what you wanted or needed to hear. I stopped knocking. I tried to ignore any sounds you produced behind your door. You continued with your letter, you continued by means of your letter, and here I am on my way to New York.

The first thirty kilometres on the 401, all I could think was how lonely I felt. After another I started to laugh, because I was exactly where I wanted to be, driving with hundreds of others through the ruined countryside, the sterile suburban sprawl, driving straight forward with no reason to stop.

It isn't my company you want right now, Beatrice. That's the impression I get. Ulrike

Huguenot. First Gustave and now his daughter. From Gustave you wanted to find out something. I'm not sure what; perhaps if a perfect love could exist between two people? But at heart you knew, I think, that he couldn't give you the answers you were after. You used to be far too awake, too realistic, too observant to believe in anything masquerading as perfect, as absolute. But now everything's changed. You don't want what's real. Why choose Ulrike to write to? You hardly know her. I get the impression you want some Ulrike of your imagination to be real, more solid than the world Ines has been torn out of, the world I inhabit, the present.

I couldn't stand the emptiness of our house. This room is no better, but it's where I've landed for the moment—room number eight.

It's not only Ines I miss, but you, Beatrice.

Since my arrival in room number eight, what have I been up to? I got sick of studying the top of the hideous dresser that I'd just photographed, and I started to feel nervous. I stared out the window, telling myself to calm down. Suddenly all my energy drained out of me. I glanced at the bed and thought, If I lie down, I won't get up again. I pulled on my jacket and hat, unlocked the door and stepped out. The concrete path was well lighted. A bright bulb had come on above every door. It wasn't until I'd left the path, crossed the parking lot and reached the road that I saw there was still light in the sky. The last light of the day was gathered in the big, shapeless, pink-tinged clouds. A strong wind was stretching and moving the clouds about. The cold dove down the neck of my jacket. I thought of all those scarves hanging in our front hall, Beatrice. I started to walk. There was only the one road. It was two lanes wide, with gravel shoulders, the motel on its south side, an empty field opposite, ploughed but with nothing growing, of course. Every few minutes a car passed, the sound of its motor growing, its lights brighter and brighter, then a horrible sucking sensation and it was gone.

I kept to the gravel shoulder. I must have walked for about fifteen minutes when a strip mall appeared in the middle of the fields. The stores were all closed, but a bright, cold light was falling from a considerable height onto the parking lot, pushing back the dark fields to reveal the hard emptiness of the lot. A cluster of some six cars was parked at the foot of a tall pole surmounted by a bright blue, rectangular sign. *Nino's Place:* the yellow letters glowed even brighter than the blue. I walked towards Nino's Place.

I saw people: two men and a woman, all three young, not yet thirty years old. Nino's Place had a picture window with a view of the parking lot and the road. They'd chosen a booth in the window.

But they were too engrossed in their conversation and beer to see me. I stood on the walkway outside their lighted window and watched them.

An earring made of plastic hoops and triangles dangled from the woman's earlobe. She had a Modigliani neck. She moved her head and the earring swung against her skin. The men were seated opposite her, both blond and ruddy cheeked, possibly brothers. A car and its noise shot down the road behind me. Two, three, four more cars, then silence. I pulled on the restaurant door and it opened. I stepped into pop music, and warm air.

Directly in front of me, flamboyant tropical fish glided, pivoted and darted above a bed of purple pebbles in a large tank. The only waitress in sight was wiping a table clean, her back to me. I took another step forward, leaving the fish behind.

The thinner of the two men wore a plaid work shirt, the other had stuffed himself into a black T-shirt. The young woman freed her attention from her friends and looked at me. Her eyes were blue, large and friendly. She smiled. There were plenty of empty booths. I could have stopped staring, chosen somewhere to sit and ordered a beer, but I didn't. "What are the three of you doing alive?" That's what I wanted to ask them.

The young woman leaned forward, so that her friend in the T-shirt could hear what she was whispering. He twisted in his seat to get a better look at me. I approached their table and introduced myself as a photographer from Canada.

"Canada? I've been there," announced Mr. T-shirt.

"Whereabouts?" I asked. "Windsor? Toronto?"

"Windsor. Toronto. Yeah, I've done Toronto a few times."

I explained that I was working on a project, that it involved driving to New York, taking pictures of people on the way, anyone, people like them, that I didn't charge anything, that the pictures were to be part of a show in an art gallery. I'd send them a print, for free. Their pictures would hang in a public space, might be seen by hundreds of people; however, I qualified my promise, nothing was certain, not yet. My project was in its earliest stages. They were the beginning. I took out my wallet and placed my card on the table in front of Mr. T-shirt. In one long, deep swallow, he drained his beer glass and set it down directly on top of my card. My card lay under the damp round base. I could see it lying there. His friends and I stared down at it through the thick, distorting glass while he looked at me, weighing my reaction. I couldn't have cared less. I gave him a long, even look. Possibly, I squared my shoulders. He peeled my damp card slowly off the bottom of his glass, "Hey, man. Sorry about that."

I shrugged. "Don't worry. I've got plenty more." I was about to walk away, slip into a booth of my own and order a beer, but Mr. T-shirt had decided he'd like to have his portrait hanging in a gallery. "So, you want to take a picture of me?" he asked.

"Yes," I told him, "of you, and one of her and of him too, one of each of you." I smiled; I widened my smile to include all of them, and the thin fellow in the plaid work shirt tilted back his head and laughed.

"What's so funny?" asked Mr. T-shirt.

"Nothing, man, nothing."

Mr. T-shirt held my card up and read out loud, "Isaac Friedman, photographer, 139 Clinton Street, Toronto." He read the postal code, phone number, e-mail, everything, the whole shebang, while I stared at the back of his hand. I'd never seen so many freckles on one patch of skin.

The young woman, her hands were long, her fingernails polished a bright blue. Her face was pretty, in a nervous way. Her prettiness felt intrusive. I wanted to shout at all three of them, "My daughter was beautiful. You should have seen my daughter." I felt I was going to cry, so I fished a tissue from my pocket, turned away and blew my nose.

She slid over to make room for me in the booth, and I slipped in beside her. "Well," I said, "You all know my name now." And they told me theirs, "Casey," "Gerry," "Craig."

I thanked them for letting me join them. The waitress came and took our orders, then Craig, the skinny one in the plaid shirt, pulled out a packet of gum. Casey accepted a stick, peeled off the silver wrapper, put the gum in her mouth. Gerry and I did the same, and then we all sat there, chewing. You would have loved it, Beatrice—the sight of our jaws going up and down. In my head I could hear you reciting to Ines, "The gum-chewing girl and the cud-chewing cow. There's a difference somehow. Ah, yes, I see now. It's the intelligent look on the face of the cow."

We just sat there, chewing our sticks of gum. None of us knew what to say to each other, then Mr. T-shirt announced, "So, you're a photographer," and I told him "Yup." But I don't think my answer satisfied him. He asked me, "So, people pay you to take pictures of them? You do weddings?"

I told him that I took pictures mostly of buildings, that I usually avoided taking people because you have to ask their permission and who knows how they'll react. Tables, chairs and door frames are easier, I assured him.

"But you want to take a picture of me?" he asked. "That's right," I said. Then the waitress set down our beers and onion rings, and we all four took napkins from the metal box in the centre of the table and spat out our chewing gum and Mr. T-shirt sat bolt upright and declared,

"Okay. Go ahead, man. Take my picture."

I can see my camera from here, Beatrice. It's sitting on the hideous dresser. The three of them are inside it.

I took her, Casey, seated in the booth, head turned slightly and down, looking at her nails, her mouth curving upward in a smile. Craig-of-the-plaid-shirt stood beside the fish tank, his arms hanging straight down at his sides, shoulders back, eyes sober, ready for inspection. Gerry—Mr. T-shirt—combed his hair, tucked in his T-shirt and tightened his belt. He's grinning, as if it's his birthday; there's enough excitement in his eyes to light the candles on the cake. The milkshake maker's behind his left ear.

What shall I do with their portraits, Beatrice? I'm thinking of hanging a small sign under each one: "This is not my daughter."

You see, Beatrice, it's a good thing I've come here, to the middle of nowhere. I'd be of little use to you at home.

I've got Ines' passport with me. I'm just telling you, in case you go into her room and start looking through her stuff. I've also got her copy of *The Odyssey*. It's in Greek, and I can't understand a word of it—that's why I brought it—and her Swiss army knife, the one I gave her on her sixteenth birthday.

Are you still writing your letter? I expect you'll keep at it until you've figured out what it is you have to say, and that you won't reach that point for a while yet. Remember to eat. Put out the garbage on Thursday mornings. I don't expect I'll stay in New York long. I hope you're all right without the car? I'll call, and perhaps I'll write again. This is the first real letter I've ever written to you.

Ulrike Huguenot is in for a surprise when she receives your letter. I don't know who I'd ask to inspect my soul. Probably no one but myself, or perhaps you, Beatrice.

Love, Isaac

It has taken me an entire day to transcribe Isaac's letter for you. I've torn it out, stopped, begun again, given up, begun. I've wanted what he says to belong only to him and to me; I've wanted not to let you read certain of his words, such as *her* and *passport*, *knife* and *Odyssey*.

I want her. I miss her.

Isaac says that you are "in for a surprise." He believes I am writing to an Ulrike of my imagination, whom I want to make more solid than the world Ines has been torn out of.

Do you agree? It seems to me that to figure out what is real can take quite a while. We may know, but not trust what we know.

It took more than a year for Isaac and me to become lovers. We moved sideways like crabs toward our desire— our desire that has rolled in then out ever since, slipping away only to crash back on us. First we became friends. One afternoon, Isaac telephoned to invite me to see a film. His love affair with the woman from Oslo had derailed. He felt twisted out of shape. "And you?" he asked. I told him I was seeing someone, which was true, but that I was free that evening and would be happy to go to the movies. As Isaac and I became friends, we went cycling through the city's ravines. Yes, cycling. Toronto's ravines are deep gullies formed by various small streams and by two principal rivers that flow down into Lake Ontario, at the base of the city.

On one of our outings, as I turned to speak to Isaac, my bicycle and I sailed off the path and crashed into some bushes, where we fell over. Isaac helped me up.

"You should look where you're going."

"Do you think so?"

I was laughing. He brushed the leaves and grass from my sweater. I climbed onto my bicycle and cycled off ahead. He caught up with me. Where the ravine ended, we rode up, into the maze of streets above. Outside a coffee shop we locked our bicycles.

"I hope I'll never fall in love again," Isaac announced as we waited for the waitress to bring our coffee.

"Why?"

"It hurts too much."

"Never again?"

"Not for a long time."

I told myself I'd achieve nothing by arguing that he ought to fall in love with me.

It wasn't until we'd lived together for more than a year that I started to argue with him over why he wasn't in love with me.

I crouched with my elbows resting on the rim of the deep white tub, in which he was taking his bath, and told him he was beautiful, which he was.

"Are you in love with me?" I asked.

He looked at me with an expression of grave apology and answered, "I love you."

"But you're not in love with me?"

"No."

"Why not?" I asked.

"I don't know."

"Is there any hope you will ever fall in love with me?"

"I don't think so. But I love you."

I reached in to the warm water and fit my finger into his navel. His wet hand came out of the water, and through my shirt he took hold of my breast. We brought our mouths together.

—

The physical pleasure we gave each other, the cyclical complexity of our intimacy, this was not what I was after. I wanted a momentous finality, an absolute. I believed that Isaac and I were poised on the brink of a vastness he refused. Or perhaps it was something tiny I was pursuing, tiny and entire.

Once, sprawled on a bed in a country inn near Oldenburg, studying the dark cloth of the shirt that covered Gustave's back, I asked him, "Why don't you kiss me?" He was seated on the foot of the bed, reading the last sentences of an article, an important article he'd brought with him in his suitcase from Berlin, an article he'd not had a chance to finish reading before picking me up at my hotel. We'd walked through the entire village, then wandered along a riverbank and into a woods and back again and climbed the narrow back staircase up to our room. We'd used the staircase where we were the least likely to be seen. I wanted to know when he planned to make love to me, because there was no escaping that our being together in that room had been planned and that soon, as planned, we would not be there; and I had already made the mistake in Canada of believing we had infinite days ahead of us when we had less than one.

Gustave looked up from the last sentence of the article in his hands and said, "That is an idiotic question, and later I'll explain to you why."

He finished the article, closed the journal, set it down on the bed and asked, "Shall we go down to dinner?"

"Shall I change my clothes?" I asked.

"You may do as you like."

I went into the bathroom and put on my only dress. I owned only one "presentable" dress and I'd brought it with me.

He waited until the wine had been served and we'd both admired the room, the thick beams and the deep fireplace, the very old and slender hinges on the door of the china cabinet near our table, before he explained, "The question you asked me was idiotic because such questions destroy desire. Don't ever ask me, or anyone else, such a question again."

I smiled at him. His good advice, uttered with serious intention and authority, made me want to laugh. Did he really believe that anyone ever follows good advice?

I wanted to laugh and to kiss him, he was so visibly pleased to be on the point of eating dinner with me, however stupid a question I'd asked. His eyes were eager and his chest confident, and his lower sensual lip and his upper skeptical lip smiled in agreement.

"I'll never ask anyone ever again why they aren't kissing me," I assured him.

"Good," he said with relief. "No more questions. Now let's eat."

Because of our long walk, we were both starving. We scrutinized the menu as if it were a poem we'd been given to memorize. We drank, we ordered, we ate and we talked until there was no one else in the room but one tired waitress, until everyone else had gone home or upstairs to bed. It was our turn to go up to bed. It would be our first time to make love to each other.

The telephone is ringing.

I had to answer. Now that Isaac has left, I answer in case it is him. It was him, his voice. He is in New York, photographing the entrances to various museums. He will stay there for only a bit longer. But he doesn't know exactly when he'll be coming home. The word *home,* as he was pronouncing it, sounded solid and full of promise. What will we say to each other, when eventually it becomes harder for him to be away from here than to be here and once again we are under this roof together? Will we stand in the kitchen like two posts?

If I concentrate, I can still hear his voice clearly. I'm sitting differently in my chair now, more alertly, his words moving around inside me. He's pronouncing the word *home,* giving it a soft heaviness, savouring the circularity at its centre.

When Isaac and I were first becoming friends, we wandered from gallery to gallery. I was determined to stop working as a translator and to start exhibiting my sculptures.

The questions being asked about works of art, at that time, were for the most part questions I'd hoped to escape by leaving linguistics behind. If a sign is itself only because it is not some other sign, then how can meaning ever be identical with itself? The answer is that it cannot be. Nor is there a single sign of unquestionable meaning toward which all other signs can be seen to point. I did not want to hear this.

"Any photograph, or sculpture, or painting is a text, a web of signifiers. A 'cat' is a 'cat' because it's not a 'bat' or a 'hat,'" Isaac reminded me with a teasing smile.

"Saussure."

"Of course, and Jakobson and Levi-Strauss, Barthes, Derrida. All of them."

"Enough."

We were standing in front of Betty Goodwin's *Vest-Earth*.

I don't expect you know her work? She's a Canadian artist. But possibly you do? In one of her series she used men's vests. Some of them she stiffened with plaster, others she pressed onto copper plates that she reworked repeatedly. From these copper plates she printed images of the vests onto paper.

Her father, a Romanian vest-maker who immigrated to Montreal in the 1920s, died when she was nine.

In *Vest-Earth,* the piece Isaac and I stood facing, she'd buried four crumpled vests in layers of soil. The vests and dirt were held in place by the glass walls of a box. The top vest, in particular, appeared to be drowning. Its empty neck protruded above the soil. The other three vests had already gone under, lost their shape, been crushed by dirt and flattened against the glass. The white lining of these vests showed in places, shockingly clean. As if the vests were new, perhaps buried alive. The soil contained small stones, bits of wood.

We were staring at a cross-section of loss. Here between two plates of glass was memory, its compressed layers revealed. I thought of rocks split open to reveal time, hundreds of centuries fixed in condensed striations. I thought of butterflies pinned inside display cases. I didn't want to ask myself about language, or the instability of meaning. I wanted to go home and bury something in earth, then dig it up again. I wanted to construct a glass box and fill it, with what?

When Isaac comes home, Ulrike, I will stop writing to you. I'll clean this house from top to bottom. How good it will feel. I'll go into Ines' room. I'll sort through her belongings and decide which to keep and which to give away. It's what must be done, isn't it? A common enough task. Why have I felt so alone? Disposing of the possessions of the dead, the dispersal of what they've left behind. I'm far from alone in having to do this. When Isaac comes back, I'll go into Ines' room. But he has not come back yet.

I said I would tell you how Isaac and I became lovers, but I haven't. One Saturday afternoon I phoned Isaac and suggested we go, on the following day, to Ward's Island. Ward's Island is flat, mostly parkland, with a few clusters of houses and a school for young children. It has neither shops nor cars. It lies in Lake Ontario, separated from Toronto's docks by a mile or so of water. Ward's is connected to a second island dominated by a small amusement park, and to a third island where people stroll and picnic on sandy beaches, and swim, on those rare days when the water is judged clean enough for swimming.

Perhaps you'll come and visit me one day, Ulrike? We could go to Ward's Island together. The best is the ferry ride out.

The ferry ride never lasts long enough. The wind careens, the waves carry ducks, the colours of the lake shift with each movement of the clouds, water slips under the prow, the city falls behind like a failed idea, the wind pulls and slaps. I never want to arrive. I want to keep going.

But once you do arrive, as you must, the islands are lovely, it's true. They are peaceful, rolled-out flat under the sky. The water slides away, then comes back for what it forgot on the beach. Bicycle wheels rattle the board-walk, the poker-faced wind shuffles the poplar's leaves, the willows sway. Beyond the water the silent city waits like a postcard, a picture to write on the back of and send far away.

If you were to visit me in Toronto, when would you come? In the summer or fall? I confess, I am intensely curious to know you. The weather here is at its best in September, or in early October.

"I was at a party last night," Isaac said as we leaned against the railing of the ferry's upper deck, the islands growing larger up ahead. "I met a woman. I liked her."

"And did she like you?"

"She seemed to."

"Have you slept with her?"

"Last night."

I looked straight down into the froth. The water slapped and slapped the side of the ferry as if the ferry were a drum. The islands were moving toward us and the rhythm of the lake made Isaac's "last night" nothing compared with now.

"Was it good? Will you sleep with her again?"

"It was nice."

"Only nice?"

"I don't think she felt completely comfortable with me. And so I didn't feel comfortable either."

I leaned farther over the railing, into the breeze. The ducks were small and handsome with fine markings. They were riding the little waves that could have been waves in a crumpled sheet on a bed. I pictured Isaac dressing, pulling on his underpants, looking about for his shirt, which lay on the floor beside a chair. Where was she? Perhaps in the next room? But rather than look in the next room, I turned my head and saw Isaac standing on the deck beside me.

"What about me?" I asked.

"You?"

"Yes."

"I didn't think you were interested. Not in me. Not in that way. Not any more."

"Well, I am."

About a week later we stopped on a busy street corner

and kissed, while people dodged round us to catch the bus.

I turned twenty-eight that summer and watched as Isaac moved his possessions into my tiny, hot apartment. The apartment had windows in two directions, thank God, and we opened them all. Whenever the humid air stirred, it brushed over us. But mostly, it didn't stir. I don't recommend that you visit Toronto in July or August.

The west window overlooked a gravelled alley lined by trees, a rickety fence, the backsides of shops. The alley ended abruptly where a church wall climbed straight into the sky.

First Isaac's razor appeared. He placed it on the window ledge beside the basin. I had no medicine cabinet or bathroom shelf. Next a selection of his books arrived, in precarious stacks, organized by subject, he claimed. They stood on the floor of my main room. Our main room. I was pleased that he planned to stay. His cameras were lined up on the mantelpiece; his corkscrew arrived with a hook he attached to the kitchen wall.

And Gustave, that summer, where was he? As far as I was concerned, he inhabited a handful of surreal days spent on my parents' island, in a time when I was preparing to give the rest of my life to wrestling with linguistic theory. I'd banished him to the outer edge of my imagination. If he tried to slip closer, I caught and held him in the disillusioning light of a particular evening in Switzerland.

I've mentioned to you the boyfriend with whom I hitchhiked through Europe, when I was a university student. He and I stopped briefly in Geneva, and I telephoned your grandmother. She invited us to dinner. "Gustave and his wife, Gerda, are staying with me. They're here from Berlin for a week of vacation. They both work too hard. We'll expect you at seven. Do you know how to get here? I don't suppose you have a car? There's a bus, or shall I ask Gustave to come and pick you up?"

We got off the bus in the village of Rolle, then walked up the hillside. The narrow road twisted back and forth between terraced vineyards, and we pressed ourselves against the stone wall each time a car sped past.

Gustave and Gerda were seated on the terrace when we arrived. You were not yet born. Your parents stood and came forward; behind them grew your grandfather's roses, the ones my father had told me about. As I kissed Gustave's cheek, I could hear my father saying, "Marcel Huguenot really was quite a remarkable fellow, a physicist who spent his free time on all fours in a bed of roses. It was a tragedy he died so young. Not a tragedy in the larger sense, but terrible for those sons of his."

"How long have you been travelling? Which countries have you visited? Where will you go next?" Gustave asked my boyfriend and me. Your mother spoke very little. Your grandmother burned her finger on a serving dish and swore. A framed picture of your grandfather revealed that Marcel Huguenot was a taller, bulkier man than I'd imagined. In the photograph, he wore old-fashioned skis and a wool cap too small for his large head.

I felt that Gustave had changed since I'd seen him on my parents' island. He had become more formal, had lost some of his liveliness. It irritated me that I couldn't tell how much of his behaviour was performance and how much truly him. In Rolle, that evening, had anyone suggested that I'd again fall in love with Gustave, I would have laughed. I believed I was freed; no more complicated emotions binding me to him. Our next encounter, nine years later at the Musée de l'Art Brut, would prove me wrong.

The postman has still not come today. No word from Isaac.

Cities belong to those who cycle and walk through them. Before Ines was born, Isaac and I used to sail on our bicycles down Toronto's side streets, under the canopies of trees, past the rows of narrow brick houses. Ines was not yet imagined, not yet wanted. We talked as we pedalled. Each house boasted a small front porch. Most of the houses were awkward and plain. But this one had an arched doorway, that one possessed a piece of stained glass, an ornate gable, a round tower in the midst of flatness and angularity, an oval window. They were pressed together, but there was no one to snap their portrait. They were not beautiful.

What was beauty? We talked in bed. We talked in the

bathroom. We disappeared, each into our own work. We learned to be silent in each other's company.

A dog is barking. This dog has been barking without stopping to rest, longer than any dog I've ever heard bark. I am hungry. I am going downstairs to get something to eat.

Ulrike, the postman has brought me a postcard from Isaac. Is Isaac a coward not to be here? No more than I'm a coward to be shutting myself in this room. What form is Isaac's cowardice taking in New York? In his postcard he doesn't mention cowardice. Here is what he says.

Dear Beatrice,
How are you doing? I've spent this afternoon shooting a hedge behind the Metropolitan Museum of Art. I shot the walls of the museum as well. A drunk lay on a bench, yelling out fragments of the Old Testament. I'd finished and was walking off when he bellowed at me to come back. I turned and looked at him. "Don't forget, buddy," he called out, "it's the details that count. God is in the details." I thanked him and walked off. The details of my present include a small coffee shop where I eat breakfast every morning, an indifferent bed that I sleep in at odd hours, an abundance of visual excitement in the long,

canyonlike streets. I don't expect I'll be staying here longer than a few more days. I miss you.

Love, Isaac.

Isaac has chosen to write these words on a postcard of a late Rothko. A swath of grey above a swath of black.

One of my letters to Gustave began:

My dearest Gustave,
What news do I have? Isaac's father, who has become suddenly frail, has taken to visiting us regularly. Ines is tired of being small for her age. In every other respect she's flourishing. Yesterday we threw a large party for stuffed animals. Four bears, a cat, a wombat, three rabbits and two dogs attended. There was an unpleasant moment when the rabbits accused a bear of cheating at "pin the tail on the donkey," but the cake was quickly served and the moment passed.
My dear, I envy your watch strap—that strip of green leather wrapped around your wrist, buckled shut so it won't fall off. The watch itself, ticking against your skin . . .

Two days later, I wrote to Gustave again.

My dearest Gustave,
I want to come and see you. I want to go to bed

with you. If you agree, I will buy a ticket and come
to Berlin in April . . .

He wrote back to me, promptly.

My dear Beatrice,
I will be very happy to see you in Berlin. What joy
your letter has given me. As soon as you have
decided the dates of your trip, let me know, so
that I can arrange things here. April will be busy,
but I ought to be able to free myself for the larger
part of a weekend. Don't worry about where to
stay. I will take care of that. I confess I am excited,
full of anticipation; and I also feel that my world
has become suddenly shaky. In April the weather
will be unpredictable. It could be quite warm, but
you ought to bring a thick jacket as the winds can
be cold and rain is always a possibility . . .

Within a day of receiving his letter, I answered him.

My dearest Gustave,
What joy your letter gives me. Thank you. I will
come and see you. We must finish properly what
we've begun. We can do so only in bed. It is the
only way to put an end to this. I am very eager to
see you. I kiss you tenderly.
     Love, Beatrice

The month of March began.

"Do you mind if I go to Berlin for ten days in April?"

I rolled from my back onto my side, to face Isaac, to receive his answer. He did not answer, and so I continued to speak. "I'll arrange for a babysitter to pick up Ines from school on the days you can't, and to come on the evenings you have to be out."

"That will help."

"Will it be worse if I go at the start or at the end of the month?"

"The end would be best."

"Do you mind if I go?"

"If I mind, will you not go?"

"I don't know."

"Why are you going?"

"To visit the galleries, to see the new buildings, to be there in the middle of it all. Apparently the whole city's become a construction site."

He waited for me to continue.

"I need ideas. The wall is down. It's the right time to go."

I was lying to him. I'd never done so before. The words coming from my mouth had as their purpose to hide the truth, and I was surprised they didn't make me feel dirty but oddly weightless, as if my dishonesty were scooping out a hollow inside me. I hadn't known it would be so easy to lie, to use one truth to conceal a different truth.

"We could all go this summer. You, Ines and I."

"I want to go now. On my own. To wander about

with nothing but my sketchbook all day, to have ideas again."

"I wouldn't mind seeing Berlin myself. I'd like to check out how it's changed."

"We could go again in the summer, or you could have a turn on your own. But I want to go now. Alone."

"Where will you stay?"

"Where we stayed last time. Or perhaps some other hotel."

"Will you see Gustave?"

"I expect so. And Gerda, Ulrike and Ingrid, if they're not all too busy."

"I'm sure they'll make time to see you. Certainly Gustave will."

Of that much Isaac was certain: Gustave would make time to see me. His other thoughts about Gustave and me he kept to himself. To give in to suspicion is as much a matter of choice as is giving in to desire.

From Toronto, I telephoned Gustave at his office. There were two possible dates I might fly to Berlin.

"Choose whichever you like," he told me brusquely.

"But isn't one better than the other, for you?"

"Either one will be difficult."

"Shall I not come? It's not too late. If you'd rather I didn't."

"I gave you my answer in my letter."

"Then I'll come on April 29."

—

That night, after putting Ines to bed, I went into my study and wrote to him:

My dearest Gustave,

You don't want me to disrupt your life. I will come as a platonic friend. I will concentrate on all the platonic elements that connect us. When we spoke earlier today, I heard clearly how angry you were with me and with yourself. Perhaps I interrupted something difficult? You were at work. That's what I dislike about telephones. Tomorrow I'll book my ticket and I'll see you soon. It will be good to speak with you face to face.

I kiss you tenderly, Beatrice.

I sent my letter, purchased my ticket and waited for his reply. He wrote: "The hotel I've chosen for you is small, old and on a quiet street. Inside it has been thoroughly modernized, which is a great shame. But perhaps you will feel the presence of ghosts all the same? It's said that Thomas Mann once fainted in the foyer. I won't come to meet you at the airport, as that would be conspicuous. I will come to collect you at your hotel, however, in the early afternoon. In what frame of mind are you coming to visit me? Will your sentiments and your intentions have changed again before you arrive? There will be time to answer these questions once you are here. I am eager to see you and I kiss you, Gustave."

—

Isaac drove me to a large shopping centre where I could catch a bus that would take me directly to the airport. Ines asked me to ride with her in the back. She pulled my hand into her lap and held on to it with both of hers. "You're not going. I won't let you." When Isaac stopped the car, I bent sideways and kissed Ines. "I'll be back very soon. I love you and I'll miss you," I assured her.

"If you'll miss me, then why are you going?" she asked.

"Because I have to."

"I thought you were going to change your mind," she said. It was not an accusation but a statement of deep disappointment, and an admission. Over the past weeks, she'd been watching, listening; and she'd hoped.

"I love you. I'll be back soon."

I opened the door and stepped out. I'd made up my mind. While I pulled my one small suitcase from the trunk, Ines started to wrestle with her seat belt, tears pouring down her face. She was six years old, had never spent more than one night away from me. I shut the door, went to the front of the car, leaned in through Isaac's window, kissed him and said, "Go." He drove off.

From the gate where I was to board the plane, I telephoned home. "She's calmed down," Isaac reassured me. "She's on the sofa, looking at a book." I'd been prepared to hang up had Ines answered. I knew she must not hear my voice. "Thank you, Isaac." "You're welcome," he said.

I attempted to quiet the emotions pounding inside me, so that I might hear every note of meaning in his voice.

"I'll be back soon. I'll call from Berlin," I promised.

"Have a good trip." He spoke with the quietness of someone turning out the lights in their living room and kitchen,
in their front hall, before going up to bed, convinced that
their choice to trust in life is the only choice possible.

I arrived in Berlin on a cool, overcast morning. Inside
the small, rather plain hotel I waited in my pink and white
room for Gustave. In the early afternoon someone
knocked at my door and I opened it. Gustave handed me
a box of chocolates.

"These are for you." He glanced about the room. "It
will have to do, I suppose. Rather small. It was the last
room they had. But tomorrow a larger room will be available and you will be able to move."

"I like this room. I don't think I'll want to move."

"Really?"

"Yes. This is a pretty room. Look, if I lean from the
window I can see that tree just next door. Before you
came, some birds landed in the top branches. I was listening to them. I can look down from here and watch the
maid come and go across the courtyard with her arms full
of sheets. I'm at a perfect height."

"Very well. As you like." He paused. My wish to stay in
the small room seemed to displease him, but he moved on
to the next subject.

"How was your flight?"

(Only later did I learn that Gustave had paid in advance
for the larger, more expensive room. "The whole week is

paid in full," the manager explained to me. "Your friend is a very generous man." The manager spoke with a lisp, and once, in the small restaurant next door to the hotel, I overheard two waiters imitating him.)

"My flight was fine, nothing special. Thank you for the chocolates." I set Gustave's gift on the bed and handed him a square, flat, rather heavy package. He unwrapped it, slipped the paper and ribbon into his jacket pocket. He turned the book over, examining its covers, front and back. *Colville.* The picture on the front showed a man with a sober expression holding his hands in front of his chin in such a way that they resembled the wings of a hawk riding a current of air, suspended. The man was wearing a wedding ring and a watch. What couldn't be seen was the pistol in front of him, its handle rising inexplicably from the table toward his fingers. That part of the painting was revealed only on the back cover.

"Thank you. This wasn't necessary."

"Necessary? No, it wasn't necessary," I agreed. "But I wanted to."

"Shall we go out? I'd hoped to come sooner, but I couldn't. I have an hour or two before . . . before I have to be somewhere else. I'll show you a park that's quite pleasant. We'll be able to speak a bit."

"All right. Yes."

He drove me to the Tiergarten, where we strolled on a path between tall trees that supported the heavy sky.

"So?" he asked. "What are your plans while you are in Berlin?"

195

"I haven't any."

"None?"

"To see you. And when I can't be with you, I'll visit the museums and galleries. There's no shortage of museums and galleries in Berlin."

"You came only to see me, and perhaps to see Berlin's museums and galleries?"

"Yes."

"Ah."

The sky hung low. We came to a kiosk and your father, Ulrike, bought us each tea in a plastic cup. We sat down on a bench to drink our warm drink. The small plastic cup heated my hands.

"I thought you weren't going to come. That you'd changed your mind. That you enjoyed playing games. Your postcard, saying that your trip was definite, arrived two days ago."

"I thought you didn't want me to come. On the telephone, you sounded as if you didn't. I'm sorry you thought I wasn't coming. I don't play games. I don't like telephones either. You're at the office and busy with something, then I make the phone ring. I hate speaking to you like that. I'm sorry my card arrived late. I would never play games with you. Didn't I say I was coming?"

"Yes, you said you were coming. So, it's because you don't like to speak to me on the telephone that you've crossed the Atlantic to speak with me on a park bench?"

"Yes."

"It is difficult to speak on the telephone, I agree."

As we'd finished our tea, we stood up and continued our walk. A narrow path between two hedges led us down to the Spree. We stood on its bank and watched the ducks, the murky water flowing slowly past.

"Would you like to go to the countryside?" he asked suddenly. "We could go in the direction of Bremen."

So I was to receive what I most wanted, but in the country-side, where no one he knew could find us. Apparently, Berlin, for him, was too awkward.

"Yes, I'd like to very much," I answered.

"Good. Then I'll come for you tomorrow, shortly after eleven. We'll return to Berlin the following day, on the Sunday in the evening. Does that suit you?"

"Yes, that suits me very well."

"Now I must take you back to your hotel. I lecture from six to nine, and I must go over what I'm going to say. These are students who hold down jobs all day, and by the time they come to hear me on Friday evenings they're exhausted. I have to plan carefully how to hold their atten-tion for three hours."

He stopped his car in front of my hotel, and when he turned to me I kissed him. He kissed me in return. Then he realized I intended our kiss to continue, and he pulled his mouth away from mine. No doubt he was afraid that someone he knew might walk past.

"We must save this for tomorrow. I will try to come for eleven. If I'm late, don't go anywhere. I may be held up. I'll come as close to eleven as possible."

"Good. In that case, I won't leave with anyone else."

—

The Bremen countryside was flat but pretty. I'm sure you know how flat it is near Bremen and Oldenburg. The inn Gustave had chosen stood at the edge of a river. The water in this river moved placidly, its current a muscle barely visible beneath the surface.

Over dinner, Gustave and I emptied events from our lives like marbles onto the table between us, as if we'd collected our experiences and saved them in our pockets to someday show to someone trustworthy and now the moment had come; out they rolled, into their own surprising beauty. Did we really believe we could choose which of our experiences to keep, and which to trade or to give away? At last, we looked around us; the room was empty. Only our weary waitress remained, discreetly rearranging forks and folding napkins on a sideboard.

We'd been given a narrow room under the eaves. "The last one available," Gustave apologized. It was filled by a large bed. While Gustave went into the washroom to brush his teeth, I stood under the sloping ceiling and thought about his advice that I must never ask anyone to kiss me. Then it was my turn to use the bathroom, and when I came out, Gustave had climbed into bed and turned out the lights. I sat down on the side of the bed that he'd left unoccupied for me, took off my shoes, then my underpants, which were old and plain, pulled my dress up over my head and down my arms, dropped all that had been covering me onto a chair. I felt solitary in my nakedness and so hid quickly under the covers, beside Gustave.

"Are you frightened?" I asked him.

"Yes. A bit."

"You needn't be. Don't be frightened."

"So you're not seventeen any more? You're the one reassuring me?"

"Yes."

It was odd to look up into his face from directly beneath him, from such a new angle.

I'm tempted to say that I didn't sleep all night. But it's easy to have the impression of not having slept, when in fact one has. At some point, I curled on my side and Gustave pressed himself against me. I lay in his warmth, his arm crossing over me. We could go no further. His hand held my breast. His thumb moved in small circles. Out of these particulars a happiness formed inside me. A happiness deep as a well, at its bottom an older happiness.

Rain started to fall outside, slanting down, slapping the shuttered windows. Gustave and I lay together, breathing.

"Are you awake?"

"Yes."

"Are you all right?"

"Not at all," he said. I waited for him to continue. "I'm thinking of the hurt I'm causing." I waited. The hurt to whom? To his wife? To me? To us both? "I've failed you," he concluded, "and you must be angry."

"I'm not."

"But you will be. You would be if this went on. I didn't expect to be this way. I've certainly fantasized about you enough. I thought I could live something complicated, but apparently I can't. I don't want to think about any of this right now. I just want to be here with you." Then he stopped speaking and we lay in silence.

A while later, Gustave rolled onto his back and started explaining how men can't be counted on, that their bodies don't always behave as they wish them to.

"I'm not angry."

"But you will be."

He insisted on explaining. He went on, needlessly questioning and analyzing. In frustration, I said out loud, to the ceiling, "I could never live with you." I had suddenly imagined going home to find Isaac gone, to find, in Isaac's place, this man so determined to tear everything apart with his questions and theories, to use words to silence our two bodies.

Then Gustave stopped talking, and I was happy. The weight of his arm, my breast in his hand, the minuscule movements of the muscles in his palm and thumb. I wanted nothing else.

There would be another time, I told myself. We'd only begun. But the sound of the rain told me there would not be another time, that we had arrived where we were going, that this would be our only night together. While Gustave slept, I listened to the rain.

—

Morning came and it was Sunday. All of Sunday the sun shone, though now and then great white clouds drifted between us and the sun. But the clouds continued quickly on their way. We rented bicycles and decided to ride to the dike that holds back the North Sea. It was the first of May. Three or four people pedalled past us, leafy branches tied to the handlebars of their bicycles. Then more people. They were celebrating spring, and the rights of all workers. It was a local custom, Gustave explained. As we watched, cycling figures glided along the flat narrow roads in the distance, ringing their bells, crossing each other's paths; and we were gliding also, and I pulled the small metal tab of the bell on the handlebar of my bicycle as the people came closer, and it rang, and Gustave rang his bell also.

"They're riding from one inn to the next. Each time they stop, they'll have a drink and eat a sort of blood pudding, then ride on until they are so drunk they fall off their bicycles."

We cycled all the way to the sea, to the dike that holds back the North Sea. It was the first dike I'd ever seen. I got off my bicycle. The wall stood thick and sober and, on the other side, spread sand, and beyond the sand swelled restless, cold water. The sound of the water carried over the wall. The waves broke with an insistence different from the insistence of the trees growing at the field's edge. We leaned our bicycles against the dike and walked several yards, but the wind blowing through our sweaters made us cold.

We pedalled back across the flat countryside under the sky's blue fist. It was a closed blue. When we arrived at the inn, Gustave said, "We'll eat something and then we should start for Berlin."

During the drive to Berlin I closed my eyes. I slept off and on, my hand resting safely in Gustave's, while his free hand steered the car.

The day before I left Berlin for Toronto, he and I ate lunch together. On all the other days he'd been tied up with work. I'd received the "larger part of a weekend," as promised. He was blameless.

I devoted each day to a single museum and to walking away from that museum in any direction, stopping whenever I liked to sketch in my notebook. The larger part of a weekend was the most I would ever receive from Gustave. I was free to cry whenever the need to do so took hold of me. There was a theatre for every evening, and each morning I bought a ticket. When it rained, I raised my umbrella. Gustave had sent a fax to my hotel, indicating the time he would come to collect me for lunch.

He took me to a restaurant that was old and small. It occupied the triangle of a crossroads. We ate in the point of the room. Red geraniums grew from a copper box in the window, and outside the window the streets and build-ings waited, but not for us or for anyone in particular.

"Well?" he asked.

"What do I think?"

"Yes. What do you think of us?"

"We love each other, we desire each other, I love and desire my husband, you love and desire your wife, you and I live in different countries. There is nothing to be done. It's impossible. But we must keep writing letters to each other."

"I agree. I've been thinking as you have. We seem to have arrived at the same place."

"Yes."

In his car, outside my hotel, I started to cry uncontrollably. I got out of the car and stood on the sidewalk with my back to him and to his car until I heard him drive away. Then I turned around to see if it were true that he and his car were gone, and it was true. I walked into a small park, where I sat on a bench. Pigeons wheeled above me, and white-bellied clouds drifted, larger than any car.

In the plane that hurled me across the Atlantic, I wrote to him. "We have begun. We have waited so long. I want to be with you. If you tell me where to meet you, I'll come."

I was unwilling to accept defeat. I convinced myself we'd only begun our explorations. I wanted more. The possibility of defeat made me prepared to risk anything. "I want to be with you," I wrote. I waited for his answer. None came. I continued to wait.

—

About a month after I got home, I received his answer.

My dear Beatrice,
We have at last become friends, truly friends. You will be angry with me for telling you this, but I cannot be your lover. I don't have it in me to live a divided life. I am happy and grateful that we are friends. I have few friends. I spend too much time working and have had a talent for alienating the few close friends I've had. Ours will continue to be an epistolary friendship; and it will probably not last long enough for me to ruin it. We won't, my poor Beatrice, have time for a long friendship. Do you remember the small bandage you saw on my arm in the morning? I think that I told you it was nothing, a routine blood test. I must tell you now that I had the test done because I'd dreamed my body was full of cancer. In my dream the cancer resembled maggots; the cancer was crawling all through me. I'd never had such a dream before, never. I went to have myself examined but believed the results would indicate that I was healthy. A dream can mean many things. The morning after you and I returned from Oldenburg to Berlin, my doctor called and asked me to come in and see her. I have a cancer of the blood. I am sorry, my dear Beatrice, to have to send you such bleak news.

I didn't make more time to see you in Berlin

because I would have been terrible company. At lunch I preferred to say nothing. I don't expect to live much longer, and my last months will likely be gruelling. I see no point in telling anyone of my illness. No one besides Gerda, you, my doctors and my lawyer knows. Ulrike and Ingrid would worry, my colleagues would calculate. Neither my brother nor mother need know. Death as it approaches distorts every relationship.

I no longer have any wish to be severe with my daughters; I want to give them everything while I can, but if I'm too indulgent they will miss me excessively once I'm gone. I must try to behave with them as I've always behaved. In the next while I'll undergo the usual volley of tests to which cancer patients are subjected, followed by the usual and more or less futile onslaught of treatments. Then we'll see. I am so sorry to have to send you this grim letter. I'm unable to write any other.

I hope you do not regret your trip to Berlin. I was unable to give you what you'd hoped for. But we are, I believe, friends, and for that I'm grateful.

Despite all I've just said, I kiss you tenderly,
Gustave.

I read your father's letter, Ulrike, and I sat and looked out this same window I'm sitting in front of now. One or two people walked down the street, and a car pulled up to the sidewalk and another pulled away. I don't really remember the people or the cars, but I expect they were there. The month of June was occurring, outside. That much I do recall, and that I shut my eyes, rocked back and forth, then opened my eyes and saw, to my surprise, that outdoors the month of June was continuing to take place. I believed, as Gustave did, that his death was imminent. I wrote and told him I would be his friend.

Your father was mistaken, as you know, happily mistaken in believing he was on the verge of dying. His cancer went into remission, and he lived another seven years.

We did meet, Gustave and I, one more time. Isaac had another show in Berlin, and Ines and I went with him. We saw your mother, but both you and Ingrid were out of town. Gustave freed himself for an afternoon, and he drove me to Potsdam, where we wandered through the gardens of Sanssouci. We spoke of you and Ingrid, and of Ines. We discussed our work. Gustave was wearing black pants held up by emerald green suspenders. The spring air moved warmly. The fountains were not turned on because they were under repair. Gustave looked suddenly down at the cuff of his white shirt and apologized because he'd dirtied his cuff. The short silk scarf he'd tied formally around his neck he loosened. Already, he'd removed his jacket. It was a grey jacket with tiny black checks, and it hung over his arm. I thought that we wouldn't kiss each other, but we did.

It happened as we were saying goodbye, on a patch of grass beside a parking lot, and just as every time Gustave touched me, time broke into its various parts and dashed off, like a pack of hunting dogs released.

It was following our Potsdam encounter that I realized I was furious with Gustave. In his infrequent letters he spoke principally of politics. He spoke with an outraged, fierce accuracy of his generation's failure to create a more just world, of the desperate need for new thinkers, for ideas. At first his thinking inspired me, and then it grew wearying. I agreed with him that humanity, short-sighted and greedy, seemed bent on self-destruction, but could he see no beauty anywhere? Were these political diatribes his idea of friendship? I felt parched. It was easy to harden myself against him. For half a year I stopped writing to him. Then I accepted our friendship, and it found its rhythm. I wrote to him perhaps six letters in a year, he wrote to me during his Christmas and summer vacations.

In one of his last letters he said, "Outside the university this evening, I grabbed a quick bite to eat from a mobile food stall called Checkpoint Curry. History is a commodity for sale everywhere in Berlin. What souvenir shall I send you, an East German soldier's hat, or would you prefer a mouse pad for your computer, decorated with an image of barbed wire and a hapless citizen being shot down while sprinting for his life? You could chase him still further, with your mouse . . .

"Berlin has succeeded in liberating itself, in reuniting its two halves. I have proved less successful. I've imposed a harsh regime on myself and those nearest me. Who have I been hoping, all my life, might forgive me? And for what? Long before I met you, I'd decided I must complete myself through work. Without ideas we are nowhere. You, Beatrice, stand a chance of influencing the ideas of others. Continue to work; your work is worthwhile."

A few weeks later, your father's cancer returned; he gathered together my letters and sent them to me. In the note that accompanied them, he wrote, "These will be best off with you." Six weeks later he died, and your mother sent me a formal death announcement, printed on stiff, expensive paper, bordered in grey. It stated the exact time at which Gustave's life had ended, and named the hospital. The small, elegant card invited its recipient to attend Gustave's funeral. However, by the time I received the card, his funeral was over.

My response to your mother was circumspect.

Dear Gerda,
Thank you for informing me of Gustave's death. Your sorrow, and that of Ulrike and Ingrid, must be immense. Isaac, Ines and I send you our sympathy.
    Respectfully,
    Beatrice Mann

I could not think of anything else to say, of anything I felt I had a right to say. I carried your father's death from here to there, as if it were a box containing him, down congested streets, out into open fields and back along highways. Eventually I opened the box and saw it was empty. His voice, looks and gestures had become a part of me. I'd already absorbed my mother's death, my father's and the deaths of close friends. This letter is full of death. I apologize. I can't imagine what you will make of it.

Soon Isaac will return from New York, and I will push myself out of this room. Ines will slam the front door shut, coming in at two in the morning, and find me in the kitchen. She'll ask me what I've been doing, shut in my room for days on end. I'm not saying that Ines is not dead. She's as dead as I can bear her to be.

You and I don't really know each other, Ulrike. However, if you wish to write to me, I would very much like to hear from you.

Respectfully yours,
Beatrice Mann

Ulrike buttoned her coat and slipped the strap of her music bag over her shoulder. The air outside, thick with flying snow, seemed in a white panic. She took a step closer to the window. Large wet flakes were sticking to the glass. She pulled on her hat and glanced at her watch. She picked up her suitcase.

The letter, in its brown envelope plastered with Canadian stamps, lay on the sofa where she'd left it the night before. She could open her suitcase and pack the letter on top of her clothes, and it would travel with her, safe and dry, to Düsseldorf. On the train she could take it out and read parts of it again. She put down her suitcase, picked up the envelope and walked over to the shelf where she kept her sheet music. She slid the envelope between two folders. It was not entirely hidden. A brown edge poked out. Now, all that remained on the sofa was Darjeeling, curled in as deep a sleep as any cat ever allows himself to fall into. She reached out to pat him but stopped herself. There was no point disturbing him.

She went into her bedroom. Of Max, two extremities

showed: his head and his left foot. From under her dark blue duvet, Max's head, turned on its side and crowned by unruly blonde hair, protruded. It was pressed into the depths of her pillow. At the bottom of the bed, his pale foot stuck out. His foot seemed to not belong to him, but feet, thought Ulrike, rarely belong. She crouched down. It was definitely his—long-toed and bony, narrow at the heel, the same foot she'd felt explore her thigh in the middle of the night. She kissed the heel. With a jerk, the reverse of a kick, the foot pulled away. It was gone, under the duvet. She came round to the side of the bed. Max's eyes were closed and he was breathing heavily, his lips slightly parted. She thought how silly it is to mistake sleep for innocence. *Innocent as a child.* But children are not innocent. He looked beautiful. To her he did, and beloved. Beloved—the word presented itself and she weighed it, as she would a piece of fruit. It felt ripe, safe to bite into. He'd wake up in an hour or so, shower, dress, make himself breakfast, gather up his belongings and go home. He might or might not make the bed. By evening he was expected in Hamburg, where his brother lived. She bent down and kissed him lightly on the lobe of his ear. He continued to sleep.

She returned to the living room. She didn't need to look at her watch to know she must hurry. In such awful weather, the short walk to the streetcar stop would take her longer than usual. The trains, however, would run on time. They always did. And tomorrow Mutti would come to feed Darjeeling.

Ulrike picked up her suitcase and opened the front door. She locked the door behind her and started briskly down the stairs. She was on her way to Düsseldorf.

PART TWO

The heart alone
is voiceless. By itself, it knows
but cannot think, and so
it cannot close the door to fear.

JAN ZWICKY, "String Practice"

February 16th, 2003

Dear Isaac,

I am sorry that you came home to an utterly empty house, nothing but a scrap of paper left on the counter in the kitchen, with a number scribbled on it, telling you where you could reach me.

It was impossible for me stay in our house any longer. I'd been waiting and waiting for you or Ulrike to rescue me. Suddenly I knew I had to start sculpting again, that or destroy something. And so I came here. I suppose I also wanted to put off the moment when we'd see each other. And now there's no putting it off any longer. I'm glad of that. You've called to say you're coming to collect me. I'm very glad that you'll be arriving here this afternoon, to take me home.

—

This letter I won't be sending, though I may hand it to you. My letter to Ulrike ended of its own accord, quite abruptly. I had nothing left to say to her. I walked from room to room, upstairs and downstairs, uncertain what to do next. Ines' room I avoided. I came back to my studio and saw the letter, all eighty pages of it, in a mound on my desk. I panicked. What monstrous act of absurdity had I been engaged in? What had I brought into existence? I couldn't send such a document to someone I hardly knew. The thought of doing so made me feel nauseous. There was no point in having written any of it. It had not brought back Ines; and neither could I send it.

I stood and listened. A car drove down the street. But it wasn't you, or the car would have stopped. Not a sound came from Ines' room. I grabbed the top pages of the letter and was about to rip them up but stopped. I snatched up the rest of the letter and looked frantically around the room for somewhere to hide it all, to conceal my complete failure. A few pages slipped and landed on the floor. I crouched down to pick them up. More slipped out of my hands. The letter existed. It was, in a sense, alive. For what reason? To be sent. I went into your study and found a padded envelope. In a state of great excitement, I sat on the floor, gathering the pages together. To calm myself I breathed slowly and, like a tightrope walker, I concentrated on a single point in front of me. Ulrike will read these pages. She'll find some sort of meaning in them. They were written for her. They exist for a reason, and I must send them.

I addressed the envelope, left the house and walked to the

post office. The sorry, small brown gardens, the cramped brick houses struck me as unaccountably beautiful, each brick, each naked twig a singular, precise wonder.

It was on my walk home, without the letter, that I became frightened. What had I done? Whoever Ulrike was, she couldn't be the young woman I imagined her to be. How would she react to such an outrageous imposition? I'd committed an act of folly. I unlocked the front door and came inside. The house was silent. I climbed the stairs and went into Ines' room. For a long time, I sat on the floor, my back to the wall, and looked around me. The curtains were closed and there wasn't much light. My eyes moved from one object to the next. The movement of my eyes from object to object reminded me of how I used to slide my fingers, counting the vertebrae in Ines' spine when she was a child. I could not possibly start to choose which of her possessions to keep and which to give away. I lay down on my back, stared at the ceiling.

It occurred to me quite suddenly that her death in no way diminished her life. Her dying couldn't undo anything she'd already experienced, it could only deprive her of what she hadn't yet lived; in other words, it could only take away what had never existed. I felt relieved. I closed my eyes and slept.

I woke very stiff, my head throbbing. When I'd figured out where I was, I pulled my knees to my chest and cried until I could no longer cry. The exertion of crying had exhausted me, and I slept some more. Eventually, I woke a second time and got up. In your study I dialed the number of the hotel where you were staying in New York and asked for you. You'd gone out. I thought of telephoning a friend, but that would have meant more words. I took hold of my shirt and rubbed it between my fingers. I went downstairs, lifted a mug from the cupboard and felt its weight and shape, did the same with a bowl. I returned to your study and searched the Internet for this place, the Mulmur Artists Retreat. I'd heard of it.

Here, fir trees form a windbreak. Someone must have planted them fifty years ago or more, judging by their size. Behind the windbreak, a single electric wire keeps cows in their snow-filled yard. I saw them standing there when I went out this morning. I don't know how long they remained rooted there before going back into the barn. Their huge, wet eyes disturbed me. Such innocence demands. Demands what? Answers, I suppose.

Will you like this place, Isaac? I expect so. In any case, we won't be staying. You are coming to take me home. My room's very plain, as are all the rooms. Mine has a wardrobe, a gooseneck lamp on a bedside table, a small desk for me to sit at, one severe chair and a window overlooking the bare orchard this side of the fir trees. The walls are painted white, the floor covered, for some reason, in green linoleum. This was, after all, once a monastery. The good, if simple, food, the quiet, the company of the other "retreatants," these have all done me good. People here seem to understand about not imposing themselves. I'm the only sculptor. Two painters and four writers are here. Here, I repeat to myself, I am here.

I cry frequently, Isaac. Do you? You are right about arriving and not arriving, and that we cannot look at anything and see it for more than a few seconds. Thank you for your phone call last night. I'm glad you phoned as soon as you got home.

Is Ines here or not? Isaac, sometimes I can feel her thinking, and her heart doing what a heart does, as I walk down past the fir trees.

I've been working in a very disciplined way, getting up early, going out for a walk through the bare orchard, then down past the fir trees before breakfast. The fir trees are full of singing, hidden, birds. On days when the air is at its coldest, the birds sing differently. The blades of their voices skate on the air until you step close. Then the sounds open, and you can hear their heat and their liquid quality.

Has a letter come for me from Ulrike? Not yet, I expect. I am prepared for the fact she may not write back.

I'm working on a large piece. It involves water, and vessels held at various angles. The smallest vessel is the size of a walnut shell; the biggest, two feet long. Some I've carved out of pieces of wood, others I'm building with clay, a few I'm weaving, using strips of cloth. The woven ones drip, of course, which is fine so long as I place them correctly.

I want to have the water fall from one vessel into the next, forcing certain ones to tip and pour, others to overflow. At the end, the water must fall one drop at a time, to strike a single spot on the ground. That is my aim.

I'm still working on the individual vessels and experimenting. Everything I've made so far can easily be dismantled and brought home. An hour or two from now, Isaac, we will be together again. What will we find out?

The air outside my window is filling with snow. It is good to be here, the world outside growing white, and me knowing that soon you'll be here. The orchard has just disappeared. The fir trees will go next. The stains on this page are not from tears but from snow that blew in a moment ago, before I could shut the window. I love you.

Beatrice

Ulrike Huguenot
Chodowiecki Strasse 42
Berlin 10405
Germany

Ms. Beatrice Mann
139 Clinton St.
Toronto, Ontario
M6G 2Y4 Canada

February 14th, 2003

Dear Beatrice,

I'm writing to you from Düsseldorf, where I'm spending a few days giving a recital, Bach and Schubert, and teaching. There's a festival on. I'm answering you from here because I want you to know, right away, that I've received your letter.

I'm very sorry to learn of Ines' death. I remember her quite clearly: a four-year-old child, concentrating on her drawings, playing in my parents' living room. I'd fixed her in time. You're right that my sister and I found her intriguing, that I did in particular. Ines made a strong impression on me. She had intelligent eyes. I was sure the world inside her head was a more interesting place than my parents' living room, where my father's moods determined how easily the rest of us could breathe.

When I opened your letter, I felt offended. You wanted something from me; and besides, your descriptions of your sexual desire for my father made me uncomfortable. I suspected you knew they would. I was surprised you'd chosen me as your confessor. I believed you didn't even know me; and later in the letter I imagined that you did, which was almost more disconcerting.

"Is this a courageous or a self-indulgent letter?" That's what I wanted to know. I couldn't decide, so I kept on reading in order to find out.

I've left your letter in Berlin. I was tempted to bring it with me, but at the last minute I didn't. I had a lot to carry, and I wanted to get away from it.

I hope my mother doesn't find it. She's looking after my cat while I'm away. I hid your letter quickly, in amongst my music on a shelf in the living room. I wanted to protect my mother. It's unlikely she'll come across it. But if she does, and admits to having read it, I'll be spared having to decide whether or not to continue hiding what you've sent me.

—

That evening on Nürnberger Strasse, the one you keep returning to, I was fourteen, but I believed I was much older. My father, as you admit, was very serious. A cloud of dark concern about the world hung over him. It hung over me.

You may confess that my father's pessimistic outlook wearied you in the long run, but you never lived with him. Have you ever walked through a field of mud? With every step your boots become heavier. The field clings to your feet. You have the impression you are lifting and trying to carry the entire field. I think you did know my father quite well, but in a limited way.

At first, as I read your letter, I assumed that honesty was not really what you wanted from me. Most of us think we want to know the truth. But I find that much of what is true is unbearable. Expressed in music, the truth is more bearable. By the end of your letter, you'd convinced me it is the truth you're after.

When your letters to my father first started arriving, my sister, Ingrid, and I treated them as a joke, and he played along.

"This is for you," Ingrid would announce, handing him the envelope. "It's a fat one."

"Yes," he'd agree.

"What does she say?" we'd ask.

"That so much snow has fallen she can't open her front door."

"No, she doesn't. You haven't read it yet."

"That's what she always says, 'The snow has piled so high I have to climb out my upstairs window.'"

"Open it."

"No."

"What else does she say?" Ingrid would ask.

"In summer, tiny black insects attack the corners of her eyes, they fly up her nose and into her ears."

I reached out and snatched your letter from his desk.

"Put that down," he ordered me. The humour had drained from his eyes.

I adored my father when I was a child; as a teenager I found him didactic, self-deluded and intolerable. I'd challenge him, "If you care so much about the poor, why don't you go work in a soup kitchen or in a shelter."

His eyes would harden. "Do you think it's so simple?"

I was ready with my answer. "I think that hiding in your university office, concocting elaborate theories, does no one any good, least of all you."

"Perhaps," he'd reply fiercely, "you shouldn't criticize what you don't understand."

"I understand how it feels to be bludgeoned by moral monologues."

"Those of us who haven't the talent to be musicians must settle for less satisfying means of contributing to the ugly world we live in. Not everyone's in a position to produce beauty."

"Are you saying I should stop playing?"

"I'm acknowledging that I must be a difficult person to live with."

He'd drop his angry plea for sympathy right in my lap, just as he walked out of the room and shut himself in his study.

If he was offering an apology, it was one I couldn't accept—not at that moment.

He died, as you well know, when I was twenty-two. I often wonder, if he hadn't kept from us, from Ingrid and me, the fact that he was ill, would he and I have fought less? In the end we reached a sort of peace. We even enjoyed each other's company. But we didn't forget the nasty things we'd said a few years earlier. We both prided ourselves on the accuracy of our memories. We did not forget.

He chose not to tell the truth, concerning his illness, and my mother went along with him. Where did that leave Ingrid and me? Protected from harm for as long as possible. There are days when the nobility of his choice, his generous determination to spare us, makes me want to cry.

But to you he spoke the truth. I will always be a bit jealous of you.

I'm glad you recognize that it isn't up to me to judge you. I am tired of finding myself in the role of judge. My father the villain, my innocent mother. My mother the villain, my father the innocent. Your letter's helped me realize I'm no longer willing to play at being judge.

—

I remember quite a lot about the evening you came to dinner, with Ines and with your husband, Isaac. You describe my mother giving you advice about Ines' eating habits, telling you what a difficult eater I was until I became envious of my friends' breasts. Well, my mother's at last given up urging me to eat, though she does bring me, now and then, small gifts of food. As for what she says about me to her friends, I don't know what stories she tells these days.

You ask if your account of Ines' birth offended or troubled me. It didn't. Though my mother's a good mother, I definitely don't want to be anyone's mother. I prefer what I can rehearse. I rarely play as well as I hope to, but at least I don't hurt anyone irreparably by my playing. My father's pessimism shackled all of us. If I had a child, I'm sure I'd tell her, or him, repeatedly, that the world is going "to hell in a hand-basket." (Is this a real expression? I read it in a murder-mystery novel I took with me on the train to Düsseldorf, to help me keep up my English. Your German, by the way, is impressive.) If I had a child, I'd become like my father. Or like my mother. It would be difficult to be myself. Or perhaps I'd discover who I really am and not be pleased. In any case, I've no plans to have a child.

You remember my mother as dressed all in white, but I don't think she often wore white.

My mother all in white? I don't think so.

A month ago, while travelling from Rome to Florence

by train, I fell into conversation with a young man. His name was Piero. He asked where I lived and I told him, Berlin. "Oh," he said, "Berlin's my father's favourite city."

"Really?" I asked.

"Oh, yeah. He adores Berlin."

"But Italy," I argued, "has fabulous cities."

"For him Berlin's special. He lived there when he was young."

Piero offered me a candy wrapped in colourful paper and I took it, though I don't really like candies. Trains are places where the unexpected is meant to happen, so I accepted his candy. It tasted of sugar, strawberries and chemicals. Piero told me that he earned his living by reading gas meters, but that his passion was mountains.

I asked if his father also loved the mountains. Families and their orchestrations, the way that elements arrange themselves to form a whole, fascinates me.

Piero laughed. "He's nuts about the mountains. They're the one thing my father and I have in common. Mostly I disappoint him. He hoped I'd be a good student. He's a professor of zoology. That's why he went to Berlin; he was offered a chance to do research. He was young, and hadn't met my mother yet. He fell in love with a Berliner, a zoologist at the same university. She was several years older than him and married. They had an affair. He tried to convince her to leave her husband, but she wouldn't. She had two young daughters."

I asked Piero if his father had told him anything else about this woman in Berlin.

"I was sixteen when he told me about her. It was a very bright, hot afternoon, so hot I'd taken a shower in the middle of the day. I thought both my parents were at work. I wandered into the kitchen in my towel, and there was my father. We started talking about nothing in particular. Suddenly he was going on about this woman, Gerda, in Berlin, and couldn't stop."

I wonder what sort of expression I had on my face, Beatrice, when I heard Piero actually say my mother's name?

"Have I said something I shouldn't have?" he asked.

"No, no." I shook my head, as if swaying my head slightly from right to left might realign its contents. "Please, go on."

As another village, then several industrial warehouses sped past our compartment window, we came to the rather obvious conclusion, Piero and I, that his father and my mother had been lovers. They'd had their affair, according to our calculations, when I was around four years old, and Ingrid, two.

At the Florence station I had to hurry, since I was playing that same evening. As for Piero, he was met by the relatives of a friend he'd come to visit in the hospital. Piero and I shook hands, then walked off, each in our own direction. That evening the concert was very well received, and the following morning I took the train home. I felt pleased with my trip. Riding along, Berlin getting closer, I asked myself if and when I'd tell my mother about my encounter with Piero. I still haven't done so.

There's a small chance that Piero and I are mistaken, that his father was in love with some other Gerda, who resembled my mother and taught zoology at the same university she did, in the same year. But I doubt we're misleading ourselves.

It's exciting to have a secret. I look at my mother and think, I know something about you that you don't know I know. It's also awkward and stands between us. But so much stands between us. If I were to tell her about Piero, we'd soon find ourselves discussing you. And now you've sent me your letter. My mother and I have a lot to discuss.

On the train home from Florence, thinking about what I'd just learned from Piero, it struck me that all my life I'd been looking at my mother through the wrong end of a pair of binoculars. All I had to do was turn the binoculars around, and the small, distant woman she'd been would grow ten times larger. I felt disoriented but freed, less tightly tied to my assessments, briefly excused of my responsibilities. Why continue to pass judgment on my parents when, clearly, I knew so little? But I'm Gustave's daughter and don't give up easily. Lately I've been observing my mother, preparing a new assessment of her, of Gustave and their marriage; and now your letter has arrived, asking me to judge you.

I once read one of the letters you sent to my father. The envelope unsealed itself as I threw it down on his desk. I threw it because I was fed up. The glue holding down the flap gave way. Your letters were thick. Sometimes you took the precaution of taping the envelope shut, but this time you hadn't. After I'd read your letter, I couldn't decide what to do. I considered leaving it, in its inviting, unsealed envelope, for my mother to find on the kitchen counter. If I left it on my father's desk, unsealed, he would ask who'd brought his mail in. Possibly he'd catch me alone. I decided to tape it shut, to say nothing to my mother. But I was not at all sure that I'd made the right decision. For several days my stomach hurt and I ate very little. This made my mother anxious. I broke down and confided in Ingrid. She very much wanted to tell Gerda; however, I insisted we shouldn't.

Ingrid and I have always been different from each other, though when we were small we were close. Every summer, our parents took us to the Alps. We stayed in the house where my mother had spent her summers as a child. We drank water from a spring, and the wind almost never let up.

Many families spend miserable vacations together. Mountains, or lakes, or even an ocean can't cure all ills. But Ingrid and I were happy in the mountains. We got up early together. If rainy weather set in, the two of us cut up old magazines and made collages, we knitted together, we reorganized our rock collections, we read each other's books.

Why didn't we spend those damp, dark days learning to hate each other, while the water gushed from the spout at the side of the house, and the trunks of the trees darkened, and the rocks became slick and the sky sagged? I have no answer.

In the city, our relationship, mine and Ingrid's, was more strained. Ingrid envied my musical ability and determination, while I envied her sociability. As I got older, I became reluctant to go to the mountains for more than a few days, as there was no piano. Then my father found someone in the village, two miles below, who had a piano, and he arranged for me to practise. I hiked down every day. They were wealthy, a stockbroker from Vienna and his wife. They'd added on several extra rooms to their house in the village, but they never stayed more than a week at a time. The local woman who cleaned for them would let me in. She was instructed to do so.

Instructions can sometimes make life easier. That time I read your letter, I wanted someone to tell me what to do. I asked Ingrid for her advice, then refused to follow it. She became exasperated. When Ingrid was angry, she would often pick things up and wave them around. She picked up my metronome. "Put that down," I said. She set it down with exaggerated care, then with one deliberate sweep of her hand knocked it over the edge, so that it crashed on the floor. Its little door fell off. "Your precious metronome. I wish you hadn't told me anything. Why did you? You don't want my advice. You think you know what's best for everyone, including Mutti. I have better things to do than to open Vati's letters and read them." She pulled on her coat and went out to join some friends.

But when my father came home that evening, she

glared at him. I was afraid she'd tell him what I'd done and what we knew. Would you like to know what you said in that letter, Beatrice?

You said that you would never forget the light that fell on the fields as you cycled with my father to the North Sea, and the cold wind that blew through your sweater when you reached the dike and the crashing of the sea from behind the dike, you'd remember it all. You weren't angry, you said, that what happened between you and my father in bed was not what either of you had expected. You wanted more than anything to see him again, and soon.

In the weeks that followed, I speculated about what exactly had happened between you and my father in bed. Whatever had occurred, I felt I was carrying the corpse of my parents' marriage draped around my neck. Only my mother, I told myself, didn't know her marriage was dead. You knew, Gustave knew and so did I; Ingrid was pretending indifference. That's what I believed. The corpse began to stink. I couldn't figure out why everyone was going about their business as usual, and I wondered how on earth I was going to bury the corpse. I stared at my sheet music, and for the first time the orderly patterns and progressions of notes held no meaning. They were nothing but a screen concealing chaos, and the chaos a screen concealing emptiness.

I stopped playing for two weeks and ate very little. My mother began to question me. "Why aren't you playing?"

"Is something wrong?" To put her off the scent, I made myself practise.

Music gradually won back the territory it had lost. I was forced to admit the beauty of many compositions. But all human relations I viewed with considerable skepticism for a long while.

I didn't dare tell my mother what I knew. I didn't read any more of your letters.

For all I knew, you'd come soon to see Gustave again. If you could fly across the Atlantic once to see my father, then you could do so twice, three times. I asked myself when my father would announce he was leaving us, to live in Canada. But he never made such an announcement.

Perhaps I hoped he would. I was fifteen and listening for tremors, dreaming of lava and destruction. My head was full of ideas about death, beauty and suffering. Death was an idea.

You are not responsible for Ines'death. You know this but want to hear me say it. Apparently it's important to you that I should be the one to absolve you. I can only speculate why this is.

As for my family, your letters contributed to our secret-iveness. However, if you'd sent none and hadn't come to visit Gustave, we would have been, all the same, a family that hid a great deal from each other. Gustave's nature was distrustful.

I resemble my father. Your letter has affected me in a way I find surprising. In the course of twenty-four hours, it has brought me closer to my boyfriend than I'd thought possible. Either I trust Max, or I don't. I can go on demanding that he prove himself, or I can accept him. He wants us to live together. I'm hard to live with, and I like my solitude. But I'm going to try moving in with him. I've decided to risk it. Your letter has helped me come to this decision. What the outcome will be, of our experiment, mine and Max's, remains to be seen.

Shall I tell my mother you've written to me? My other choice is to protect her. It is almost two in the morning, and my ability to think is fading. I've said more than I should.

You've asked me for my friendship. The best answer I can give is that we are starting to know each other. You were Gustave's friend.

I hope your husband, Isaac, has come home. I wish him well.

Thank you for writing to me, Beatrice. Your letter contains so much of my father.

Respectfully,
Ulrike Huguenot

Beatrice read Ulrike's last paragraph again, folded the letter and put it away with Gustave's and her own in the yellow metal box decorated with a caricature of a turbaned Moor. The lid was difficult to fit in place, the box being more than full. She returned the box to its shelf, left her studio, crossed the hall and opened the door of Isaac's study. He was working at his computer, examining shots of the back wall of the Metropolitan Museum of Art.

"Any good ones?"

"Quite a few, actually. Are you going out?"

"Just for a walk."

"Will you be gone long?"

"An hour at the most."

She was about to leave, but instead she bent down and kissed him on the mouth. Then she pressed her nose behind his ear and smelled his skin.

Through her sweater, Isaac felt the comforting solidity of Beatrice's hip under his hand. He pulled her as close to him as possible before letting his hand fall.

She went down the stairs and saw her coat. It was hanging, with its full weight, from one of the hooks in the wall. Beside her coat hung Isaac's. Their boots stood on the floor. She took down her coat and pulled it on, tugged on her boots and saw that salt from the street had stained the toes with a white powder. She opened the door and stepped out. She walked past the small, barren front yards. Overnight, all the snow had melted, as if winter were finished. She could have worn shoes instead of boots. She considered going back but didn't. If the unusually mild weather continued, the trees would be fooled into putting out buds. She unbuttoned her coat as she walked.

ACKNOWLEDGEMENTS

I would like to thank the following for the help they gave me during the writing of this novel: Jennifer Glossop, Jan Zwicky, Kyo Maclear and Joy Gugeler for pivotal insights midway through; Modris Eksteins, Liz Warman, Marylin Lerner, Liz Acker, Sarah Winters, Doina Popescu, Inge Ali, Carrie Whitney-Brown, Jeff Whitney-Brown, Heidi Schaefer, Susan Glickman, Geneviève Guillot, Christophe Dejours, Desmond Morton, Alexander Freund and Charles Egger for coming to my rescue with knowledge and twists in perspective; Theo Heras and Joanne Schwartz for a choice of quiet rooms; Gilda Rippen for unforgettable times spent together in Germany; Anne Egger and Greg Sharp for being themselves; the staff at the Parliament Library for their support.

Special thanks to photographer Vid Ingelevics for years of challenging conversation and for allowing me to draw from his work, in particular from his piece *alltagsgeschichten (Some*

Histories of Everyday Life), on which I closely based the DP project attributed to Isaac in this novel. I was also inspired by the art of photographer Shimon Attie. Beatrice's tire sculptures are an interpretation of a piece titled *Retreads*, by sculptor Colm McCool.

In Alexandra Richie's informative and engaging *Faust's Metropolis: A History of Berlin* (Carroll & Graf Publishers, 1998), I found answers to many of my questions.

The generous support of the Canada Council for the Arts gave me faith in this novel and much-needed time to write.

Hats off to my agent, Samantha Haywood, and my editor at Knopf, Kendall Anderson.

As always, my sister, Christina MacCormick, offered me invaluable insights and encouragement. Finally, I thank Emma and Jonno.

The Berlin in this novel is a fictitious Berlin. A few of the street names may not appear on any known map of the city.

MARTHA BAILLIE was born in Toronto. Her poems have been widely published in journals such as *Descant, Prairie Fire* and the *Antigonish Review*. Her first novel, *My Sister Esther,* was published by Turnstone Press in 1995. Her second, *Madame Balashovskaya's Apartment,* was published by Turnstone Press in 1999 and then published in Germany and Hungary. After time spent in Edinburgh, Paris and Asia, Baillie returned to Toronto, where she now lives.

A NOTE ABOUT THE TYPES

The Shape I Gave You is set in *Mrs. Eaves* and *Adobe Jenson*.

Mrs. Eaves is a modern face designed by Zuzana Licko of the American digital type foundry Emigre. It draws its influences both from classic French types of the 16th century such as *Fournier*, as well as mid-twentieth versions of the classic English text face *Baskerville*.

Adobe Jenson is based on *Antique Jenson*, a modern face which captures the essence of Nicolas Jenson's roman and Ludovico degli Arrighi's italic typeface designs. The combined strength and beauty of these two icons of Renaissance type result in an elegant typeface suited to a broad spectrum of applications.